Bony Buys a Woman

Arthur Upfield was born at Gosport, Hants, in 1888, and emigrated to Australia at the age of 23. In the First World War he served in the Australian Army. Afterwards he roamed Australia, learning all the minor miracles of Australian life. In turn he worked as a boundary-rider, offside driver, cattle-drover, rabbit-trapper and manager of a cattle station. He got to know the Aborigines and their customs, many of which appear in the 'Bony' novels. His half-Aborigine sleuth, Detective Inspector Napoleon Bonaparte, is based on a character he knew well. He had written fifteen books before he was first published in 1951, since when many 'Bony' books have appeared. And, though success came late, it was considerable, enabling him to live in comfort in New South Wales until his death in 1965.

Also by Arthur Upfield in Pan Books

Arthur Upfield

Bony buys a woman

Pan Books in association with
William Heinemann

First published 1957 by William Heinemann Ltd
This edition published 1959 by Pan Books Ltd,
Cavaye Place, London SW10 9PG
in association with William Heinemann Ltd
6th Printing 1975
ISBN 0 330 10586 8

Printed in Great Britain by
Richard Clay (The Chaucer Press) Ltd, Bungay, Suffolk

ONE

A BEGINNING FOR LINDA

THE DAY was the 7th of February, and it was just another day to Linda Bell. Of course, the sun was blazing hot at six in the morning, another morning when the wind sprang up long before six and was a half gale when the sun rose. It sang when crossing the sandy ground, and roared farewell as it sped through the line of pine trees guarding the Mount Eden homestead from the sprawling giant called Lake Eyre.

For Linda this day began like all other days. First she slipped from bed and gazed at the large calendar on the wall above the dressing-table. Later she would be asked to name the day, and already she knew that to remember it would be conducive to happiness.

Linda was most self-dependent although she was only seven years old. She needed no rousing, no instructions on how to begin a new day. Taking a towel from a rack, she tripped daintily through the open french windows to the veranda, and along the covered way to the shower recesses. She sang a little song to the accompaniment of the wind under the iron roof as the tepid water from the great tanks high above the ground sluiced down her white body. Now and then into the song crept the word 'seven', and the same word occurred when she was still singing, on regaining her room and proceeding to dress. She was making her bed when the breakfast gong without defied the wind, to call the Boss and the Hands.

The homestead kitchen was large, already hot, filled with the aroma of coffee, frying mince-balls, and grilling steaks. At one end stood the small table where Linda and her mother ate, and at the other end was the annexe in which the men ate. The men appeared and sat at the long table, and Mrs Bell asked each what they chose, and served them. That done, she served a cereal to Linda without consulting her, and then carried Mr

Wootton's breakfast tray to the inner dining-room.

Mrs Bell was plump, fair, thirty, and pleasing to behold. It was said that her husband was a horse trainer, and that she had once been a school teacher. She believed that children were no different to horses – that they needed to be trained with firmness and kindness, and that if training is left too late, the child becomes a useless adult, precisely as belated training is wasted effort on a horse or a working dog. Thus she spared herself no trouble, but saved herself much worry.

'You have done your hair nicely this morning, Linda,' she observed as she sat at table with her daughter. 'Saves time to do it nicely in the first place. What is the date today?'

'February Seven, One Nine Five Seven,' intoned Linda, her grey eyes wide and faintly impish.

'That's my girl,' approved Mrs Bell. 'Mr Wootton says he's going to town today, and I see that your comb has lost two teeth. What colour would you like the new one to be?'

Linda chose blue, but her mind was on the slight noises made by the hands leaving the meal annexe. Her mother asked her to tell the time by the wall clock.

Hurrying now to finish her breakfast, Linda's jaws slowed while she gazed at the clock. Then she guessed a little, as she always found it difficult to be sure whether before or after the hour. This morning she guessed correctly by answering:

'Seven minutes to seven, mother.'

'Good for you, Linda. Now I suppose you want to run out to see the men off to work. Well, you may go. When the men have left, come in and do your lessons. It's going to be a nasty day, and we'll get through as quickly as you've a mind to, shall we?'

The homestead buildings at Mount Eden formed the sides of a large square. The main house occupied the east side, the men's quarters the side opposite. On the flanks were the office and store shed, the horse yards, the trade shops, the well and reservoir tanks. In the corner of the square was a round house, constructed entirely of canegrass.

When, a trifle too hurriedly, Linda said grace and skipped from the kitchen, she stepped right into the open square.

Already the early morning shadows were deepening in sharp contrast with the sunlit ground, and squadrons of dust horses ridden by riders of the west wind were racing from the men's quarters to the house, passing by and speeding up the slope to the line of pine trees and the vast open Lake Eyre beyond them.

The men were coming from the quarters to receive their orders for the day. There were four, all white men. Three wore spurs on their riding boots. One was a heavy man, two were lean, and the fourth a young man darkly handsome, and, compared with the others, almost flashily dressed in the ultra-stockman style.

They halted just outside the office door. The young man waved to Linda, and the big man called the morning greeting. Then Mr Wootton appeared from the house side veranda. He was short and stout, red of face, when the complexion of his men was uniformly nigger-brown. His clipped moustache was dark. His hair was worn short and was plainly grey at the temples. His eyes were small and distinctly green, and always kindly for Linda. To her he was the Big Boss, the King of Mount Eden. Unfailingly he must be called 'Mister Wootton'. Invariably he wore a soft-collared shirt and a tie, gabardine trousers and shoes, instead of riding boots.

As usual, Mr Wootton slipped a key into the office door lock and entered. He was invisible for two to three minutes and Linda knew he was studying a big book kept on his desk, and knew, too, that he looked into the book to tell him all about the station, and what needed to be done. On reappearing, he stood in the doorway and called for Arnold.

Arnold was the very large man who could do anything from blacksmithing to making a motor engine go. Because of the wind and the cawing of passing crows, Mr Wootton had to speak loudly.

'Want anything from town today, Arnold?' The big man shook his head, saying:

'Don't think so, Mr Wootton. Not for the station, anyway.'

'All right. The wind oughtn't to be strong out at Boulka. You might take the truck and go for another load of iron. And

7

take your time to get the iron off without tearing holes in it. You know.'

'Good enough,' drawled Arnold, and Linda asked:

'May I go with Arnold, Mr Wootton?'

'If your mother says so,' he assented, and called Eric.

Linda raced to the house. Eric was lanky, raw-boned, slow. When Linda returned he was saying:

'The mud'll keep 'em from crossing for another six weeks even if it don't rain, which ain't likely. Them steers know enough to shy off getting themselves bogged. 'Sides, before the lake is hard enough to take 'em, the flood oughta be right down the Coopers and the Georgina, an' spilling over from the Diamantina.'

'Could be, Eric,' agreed Mr Wootton. 'Well, take a ride out to Number Fourteen and look over the stores. Anything you want from town today?'

Eric chuckled dryly, and winked at Linda.

'Well,' he drawled, 'you might bring me a box of them lollies with the nuts on 'em. Seems like I got to give a present to my girl. Must keep in with her, y'know.'

'Yes, you must get a present for your sweetheart,' agreed Mr Wootton, seriously. 'Is her name Linda, by any chance?'

'That's tellin', Mr Wootton,' and again the wink which produced beaming adoration in the little girl's face.

The next man called to receive orders was the young man named Harry. He came forward with rolling gait, and even the wind could not drown the tinkle of his spurs. He was sent out to ride a section of the boundary fence. The fourth man, named Bill, was instructed to ride into White-Gum Depression and report on the feed. To him Mr Wootton put questions concerning the aborigines.

'Any sign of Canute and his people, Bill?'

'Sort of local? Naw, Mr Wootton. They're never to hand when wanted. They'll be away up on the Neales by now, living on lizards and ants, going for corroborees and such like, and putting the young fellers through the hoop.'

'Charlie promised he would come back early to give a hand with the muster.'

8

'You'll see Charlie when you see Meena. And that'll be when Canute says so. He's their boss. You can send 'em to the Mission Station, teach 'em to read and write and sing hymns, but in the end they do just what old Canute tells 'em.'

'Yes, yes, I know,' Mr Wootton agreed explosively. 'All right, Bill. Want anything from town?'

'Well, you could bring me a coupla pairs of them grey pants you got me last winter. Oh, an' what about a couple of ladies' handkerchiefs? Small ones with lace round the edges, and the letter 'L' in the corner. The store'll have them kind. I got a sort of sister called . . . why, hullo, Linda, I didn't see you.'

'You did so, Bill,' argued Linda, from whose face disappointment had been banished by joy.

'Oh, Linda!' said Mr Wootton. 'Will your mother allow you to go with Arnold?'

'Mother says not to, Mr Wootton. Mother says I have to stay and help her because Meena and the others are still away.'

'I didn't think of that, Linda. Of course you must help your mother. All right, Bill. I'll not forget the handkerchiefs and the box of nut chocolates.'

Mr Wootton re-entered his office, and Linda accompanied Bill to the yards, where the other riders were saddling up. She watched them leave, and then went back to the house, and demurely dried breakfast dishes for her mother.

After that, lessons at the kitchen table until nine o'clock, when Mrs Bell sounded the house gong, made tea, and provided buttered scones. Mr Wootton came to the kitchen for morning tea, standing the while, and noting on a pad the items Mrs Bell needed. Linda accompanied him to the car shed, and stood watching as the dust and sun-glare took the car up into the sky over the track to Loaders Springs.

She was now free for the remainder of the morning, free to be herself, free to chide and scold and love, instead of being chided and loved. There beside the car shed was her own circular house, a circular house having canegrass walls and a canegrass thatched roof, and a wood floor three feet above ground to keep the snakes and ants out; a little house for a little girl, built by the girl's sweethearts.

9

Thus far, just another day for Linda Bell.

She ran up the two steps and through the thick grass doorway to enter her house, leaving the buffeting wind outside, and meeting with calm silence. There was a real window set in the thick grass wall, and the window faced to the south, from which the cool winds of winter came. There was a table with the legs shortened, and a chair with the legs shortened. There was a rough bookstand and real books on the shelves, and on top of the stand were four dolls.

One doll was the exact likeness of her mother. Another was the image of Mr Wootton. The third was a lovely young woman with straight black hair and large dark-brown eyes, and the fourth was an elderly man with weak blue eyes, a long face, and drooping grey moustache.

Linda stood before the dolls, and said:

'Meena! What's the date? No, it's not February 10th, Meena. You should know the date. You went to Mission School. All right, Ole Fren Yorky, you tell me the date. February 9th! Of course it isn't February 9th.' Linda glared at the doll with the weak blue eyes and the absurdly drooping grey moustache. She mimicked her mother: 'Ole Fren Yorky, I'm asking you to tell me the date today. Oh dear! Won't you ever learn!'

So the conversation with the four dolls continued over a wide range of subjects, including a box of chocolates with nuts on top, and lace-edged hankies with the letter L in the corner. She was seated in the chair, the dolls on the table before her. She had straightened Mr Wootton's tie, and had combed Meena's hair, and was intently trying to twirl points of Ole Fren Yorky's moustache when the report of a rifle obliterated the low buzzing of the blowflies.

'Now, Ole Fren Yorky, stay still,' she scolded. 'Your moustache is getting disgraceful. That'll be Mr Wootton out there shooting the crows. You know very well how naughty they are, and have to be shot sometimes.'

Ole Fren Yorky wouldn't be still, and Linda had to concentrate on gaining compliance with her efforts. Minutes later, she remembered that Mr Wootton had left an hour before for

Loaders Springs. A tiny frown puckered her dark brows. She pushed Ole Fren Yorky to one side; and had put her hands to the table to push her chair away from it, when there appeared in the doorway the original Ole Fren Yorky.

Terror leaped upon her. The man's weak blue eyes were now hot and blazing. He ran forward, a light swag at his back, a rifle in his left hand. Linda sprang out of the chair, and then found herself unable to move. A bare arm gripped her about the waist and she was lifted. She opened her mouth to scream, and her face was pressed hard into a sweaty chest, and no longer was it just another day.

TWO

MURDER IN EDEN

UNTIL FOUR o'clock it was just another day for Arnold Bray.

Like many big men, Bray was deliberate in thought as well as action, and this led people to believe him to be slow in both. Under thirty, he received the respect of men of his class much older than himself, and from men much younger who noted his powerful physique.

He was that asset to all pastoral properties – the man of all trades, and it was quite unnecessary for Wootton to advise him how to remove iron sheets from a roof. The building to which he drove this day was situated some twelve miles from the Mount Eden homestead, and had been used as a shearing shed in a period when sheep were reared, only to be severely attacked by wild dogs. In this land where rust is reduced to a minimum by the dry atmosphere, the roof iron was worth salvaging.

By three o'clock Arnold had removed enough iron for a sound load, and, having lashed it securely from the high wind he would encounter on leaving this shelter amid tall blue gums, he took time to boil water and brew a quart pot of tea. It was three-thirty when he called the dogs into the truck cabin and started for the homestead.

Once beyond the trees, the wind buffeted the load and made steering on the narrow and little-used track something of a task. The truck hummed powerfully as it moved up a long and gradual slope to the summit of the highlands, which were never more than two hundred feet above the lowlands marked so clearly by creek and swamp and depression. Here on the bare slopes lay vast areas of ironstone gibbers, closely packed like cobbles, evenly laid into the cement base of earth-clay, and so polished by the wind-driven sand grains that they reflected the sunlight in a glassy glare.

Here, this day, earth and sky merged without an horizon. Arnold could not have seen the summit of the long slope had he looked for it, so masked was this world of open space and wind and dust by the distortion of sunlight. A tall solitary tree became a mere broken sapling; a boulder reached in a few seconds had appeared to be a dozen miles distant; what had seemed to be a barrier of sand was actually a faint fold in the earth.

Abruptly, in front of Arnold's truck was the homestead; the square of buildings, the line of pines, the braked windmills, all like a picture left upon the floor and covered with the dust of years-long neglect. Yet the homestead was two hundred feet below the truck, and a mile away.

The wind was blowing to the truck, a gusty wind which stockmen would find slightly unpleasant, not unbearable. The two dogs squatting on the seat beside the driver were happy until but half a mile from the homestead. Then, at the same time, both tensed, began sniffing, finally joined in a chorus of low lament.

Arnold could see Eric mounted on his horse, and the horse was standing almost motionless in the centre of the square fashioned by the buildings. The animal's legs seemed a hundred feet high, and Eric appeared to be sitting on a barrel, causing Arnold to chuckle, because never was he bored by the tricks played by this remarkable land.

Attracted by the dogs' behaviour, wondering at the stockman's most unusual stance, Arnold pressed on the accelerator, arriving at the motor shed, where the iron was to be stacked, in a cross cloud of dust and squealing brakes. Eric dismounted, and led his horse to the man standing beside the grounded dogs.

'Been hell to play,' he said, the slow voice failing to hide shock. 'No one here but her. The kid ... I can't find the kid. Mrs Bell's over by the kitchen door. I covered her up. I ...'

'What happened?' asked Arnold, his steady voice not matching the concern in his eyes.

'Don't rightly know. Exceptin' that Mrs Bell's been shot dead. The boss . . .'

'Was set to leave for town,' supplemented Arnold. 'Let's look-see. How long you been back?'

'Quarter hour, half hour, I don't know. I got to the yards and saw the crows by the kitchen door where no crows oughta been. So I rode over and saw what it was. I yelled and screamed for the kid, but she didn't come out from nowhere. And no one else either. I don't get it. I tell you, Arnold, I don't get it.'

'We will. Anchor that horse somewhere. Wait! Keep the horse. May want it in a hurry.'

Arnold glanced at his shadow, subconsciously noting the time, recalling that his employer usually returned from town between five and six. A great number of crows were circling about, dozens more were perched on the house roof and on the round roof of Linda's playhouse. What they had done to the dead woman's neck and arms. . . . It was Mrs Bell without a shadow of doubt. Arnold gently replaced the bag over the body and stared into the troubled eyes of the rider. The dogs slunk away. Eric said:

'I did right covering her? Then I got back on my horse and shouted for Linda. Got the jitters sort of. Expected someone to shoot me. What're we to do?'

'Find the kid. Where have you looked?'

'Nowhere. Just shouted. Them crows! She musta been shot this morning.'

'Take a hold, Eric.' Arnold's voice was quiet, and it calmed Eric Maundy. The slight twitching of his lips firmed to grim anger. 'We'll look-see in the house first; there's no one else around, accordin' to them crows.'

Inside the kitchen, they called for the child, waiting for her reply. Here, where the wind was baffled, the silence was hot and familiar. Their shouts fled away into the rooms beyond, to crouch in corners and wait for them. When they entered the spacious living-room they were halted by the wreckage of the expensive transceiver, and by the smashed telephone instrument. It was the first time Eric had been there, but Arnold had often serviced the telephone.

There was no further damage. Nothing had been disturbed. Eric found the axe with which the instruments had been destroyed, lying under a chair where it had been carelessly flung.

The dust was crossing the open square, tinting the buildings, brazing the hard clay ground. Above, the crows were streaking black comets against the glassy roof of white flame. Eric said:

'More ruddy crows than when we kill a beast. Blast 'em!'

Arnold made no comment, and Eric followed him in a further systematic search, beginning at the canegrass meat-house, trying the locks of the office and the store room, proceeding to the playhouse.

The four dolls were on the table, Ole Fren Yorky toppled and lying on his back. The place was in its usual tidy disorder, familiar to both men. There was nowhere here for Linda to hide. Leaving, they looked under the floor, knowing they could see beyond the structure, hoping against vanquished hope. They had finished with the men's quarters, a building containing four bedrooms and a common-room, when Arnold saw young Harry Lawton dismounting at the stockyard gates.

His shout stopped the young man from freeing the horse, brought him to them, large spurs jangling, red neckerchief flapping.

'You'll want your horse,' Arnold said. 'There's been a shooting. Mrs Bell is dead and Linda has vanished.'

'Hell!' exploded Harry. 'Linda couldn't have shot her ma. What else happened?'

'Ain't that enough?' demanded Eric, and waited for instructions from Arnold.

'You fellers get going. Ride around. Look for tracks. Look for . . . you know. Look for Linda. Somebody came after the boss left for town. The bloody crows didn't shoot Mrs Bell.'

They obeyed without question that steady authoritative voice, and Arnold went back to the quarters and leaned against the front wall and chipped at a tobacco plug. He was cold deep down in his mind, so enraged that, now no one was near to see, his grey eyes were wide and blazing.

15

The question tormented him. Who had done this grim thing? A traveller? Hardly. No tracks went beyond Mount Eden, save the little-used track to the old homestead called Boulka, and he himself had just come in by that track. A traveller was as rare as an iced bottle of beer on the centre of Lake Eyre. All the blacks were away on the Neales River, fifty miles to the north. The nearest town, Loaders Springs, was more than forty miles to the southwest, and the nearest homestead was something like a hundred and ten miles away round the southern verge of the lake.

There was left ... what? Five white men who had eaten breakfast here at Mount Eden, and any one of those men, including himself, could have returned, unknown to the others, and murdered the woman. And the kid? No ... no! That Arnold wouldn't accept. Every man of them loved Linda. Knowing he would find no tracks, Arnold yet sought for tracks of strangers, or tracks betraying unusual movement out of time.

He was trudging about the hard, sand-blasted ground when Bill Harte joined him. Neither spoke, both staring into the eyes of the other. Harte was small, wiry, bow-legged, and iron-fisted. Under the weathered complexion lay the barest hint of mixed ancestry. The tight lips parted in what could have been a snarl, but his voice was low and clipped.

'Met Eric on the way in,' he stated. 'Told me. No sign of the girl?'

'No sign of anything, Bill. You see around. You're better than I am at it.'

They walked to the body, and Harte lifted the bag.

'She was running when she was shot,' he said. 'She was running from the kitchen door, and whoever shot her was standing in the doorway. Betcher on that. Prob'ly was runnin' to grab up Linda. Linda musta been in her playhouse when it happened. You looked there, of course?'

Arnold didn't reply to the obvious. Harte moved away, almost at the run, crouching to bring his eyes closer to the ground, and the big man, watching, realized that he was a mere amateur tracker beside Bill Harte. All the others were superior to him, too, but then all of them together knew less than he of welding iron or repairing a pump.

What to do now? Something had to be done with the body. It had lain there for hours, and the ants were investigating it. Arnold judged by his shadow that it was close to five o'clock, when Wootton's return could not be far off. Harte was running about the outbuildings, like a distraught dog. The others were nowhere in sight. Yes, something had to be done beside just standing about. The boss might be late, mightn't get back till after dark.

From the carpenter's shop he brought several wooden pegs and a hammer. The pegs he hammered into the hard ground so that they outlined the body, then he dusted the ants from it, turned it over, and for a space looked down upon the pained face and the wide grey eyes in which revolt against death was so plain.

Without effort, Arnold Bray took up the body and carried it to the woman's bedroom, where he placed it on the bed and then found a spare sheet with which to cover it. Cover the Dead. . . . She had been a good woman, above him in so many things, a woman he had admired humbly when there had been women he had admired, but not humbly. The possible motive for this thing, so much worse than mere murder you read of in the papers, persisted in entering his mind, although he fought it back with savage anger. And so preoccupied was he by the futility of it all that without conscious animation he drew the blind, and then passed from room to room to draw down every blind.

Bill Harte called from the rear door, and Arnold went to him, hope reborn, and slain again when he looked into Bill's eyes.

'Come with me,' Harte said harshly. 'You check.'

He led the way to the underground tank which had cemented floor and walls and a canegrass roof rising to a pyramidal summit. From this place he proceeded a dozen steps to the rear of the meat-house, where he halted and stared at the ground against the grass wall in the lee.

'What d'you see?' he demanded.

17

Arnold saw nothing at first, save the imprints of a dog. Then larger prints appeared to grow on the light-red ground, so that the dog's prints faded into insignificance. What now he was seeing were three prints made by a man's boots. They were unusual in that there were no heel marks.

'You musta seen those prints some time or other,' Bill stated.

'If I did I don't recall them,' admitted Arnold. 'Still, they look like the prints of a man running. No heel marks. I know! Ole Fren Yorky walks like he's always running. They're his tracks.'

'Yair. Yorky made 'em.'

'But Yorky's in town on a bender.'

'Couldn't be. Yorky made them tracks four-five hours ago. That right what Eric says about the telephone and the transceiver?'

Arnold nodded. He said with sudden determination:

'I'm driving the truck to meet the boss. He'll have to go back to town to report to Pierce and bring men out to join in the hunt for Yorky. Yorky's got Linda ... if he hasn't killed her. Yorky's got to be nabbed, and quick. If he's killed Linda you keep him away from me.'

THREE

THE DECEITFUL LAND

WITHIN MINUTES of a crime being reported in a city, a superbly organized Police Department, backed by modern scientific aids, goes into action. It was not to the discredit of Senior Constable Pierce that he was thwarted by inability to see without lights over an area of something like ten thousand square miles of semi-desolation; because the weather was against him in a land where the weather can aid or baffle keen eyes and keen brains.

He arrived with the doctor from Loaders Springs shortly after nine on that night following the murder of Mrs Bell. It was then black night, the stars blotted out by dust raised all day by the mighty wind. Before dawn a new transceiver was working at the Mount Eden homestead, and a new telephone installed. At dawn two trucks left to locate the aborigines and bring back all the males, to be put to tracking. Soon after dawn cars and trucks began to arrive, bringing neighbours from homesteads fifty, sixty, a hundred miles distant, and at dawn other men rode out from homesteads still farther distant to patrol possible lines of escape for the murderer of Mrs Bell, and the abductor of her daughter.

The man called Ole Fren Yorky, born in Yorkshire, brought to Australia when he was fifteen, outwitted bushmen reared in this vastness of land and sky, and the native trackers of whom the world has no equal. His tracks were discovered at the vacated camp of the aborigines situated less than a mile from the homestead, and beside the canegrass meat-house within yards of the house kitchen door; those two places sheltered by the wind. He carried a Winchester .44 repeating rifle, and the woman had been shot by a bullet of this calibre.

Men discussed the motive, but more important was the finding of Linda Bell, alive or dead. Her fate was of paramount importance, for until the child's body was found, hope remained in the hearts of the hunters.

The initial verve of the hunters gradually degenerated into doggedness. The aborigines lost interest, rebelled against the driving of the white men, as though convinced that Yorky, with the child, had won clear of their ancient tribal grounds.

The white force dwindled, men being recalled to their homestead to attend chores which could no longer be neglected, and at the end of four weeks the organized search was abandoned.

Three days after Constable Pierce informed Wootton of the official abandonment of the search, the station owner was told of the coming of another policeman. Wootton had engaged Sarah, from the aborigines' camp, as cook, and Sarah's daughter, Meena, as maid, and the routine of the station was as though interruption had never been when this morning, as usual, Meena brought to the living-room table the large tray bearing Mr Wootton's breakfast. Cheerfully he said 'Good morning', and shyly demure as usual, Meena responded.

Meena was in her early twenties. She had lost the awkward angularity of youth, and was yet distant from ungainliness reached early by the aborigines. Not a full blood, her complexion was honey, and her features were strongly influenced by her father, even her eyes being flecked with grey. Wearing a colourful print dress protected by a snow-white apron, her straight dark hair bunched low on her neck, and with red shoes on her feet, she was an asset to any homestead, and, in fact, was appreciated by Mr Wootton. Her voice was without accent, soft and slow.

'Old Canute say for me to ask you for tobacco in advance. He's been giving too much to Murtee, and Murtee says he used his to stop old Sam's toothache.'

'Sam's toothache, Meena!' exclaimed Mr Wootton. 'Why, old Sam must have lost his last tooth fifty years ago.'

'Old Sam lost his last tooth before I was born. But old Canute's run through his tobacco. He says if Mr Wootton won't hand out, then tell Mr Wootton what about a trade.'

'A trade! Explain, Meena.'

'Canute says for you to give him a plug of tobacco, and he'll tell you something you ought to know.'

'Oh,' murmured Mr Wootton. 'Sounds like blackmail to me. D'you know what this something is I ought to know?'

'Yes, Mr Wootton. I know. Canute told me.'

'And you won't tell unless I promise to give that wily scoundrel a plug of tobacco?'

The expression of severity on the cattleman's face subdued Meena. For the first time she shuffled her feet on the bare linoleum. She spoke two words revealing the unalterable position she occupied.

'Canute boss.'

Wootton's experience of aborigines was limited, but he did know the force and authority wielded by the head man of a native clan, and thus was aware that the girl was behaving naturally, was merely a go-between as the messenger between Canute and himself. Severity faded from his green eyes.

'All right, Meena. I'll trade. Pour me a cup of coffee.'

The girl poured the coffee, then, standing away from the table, she said:

'Old Canute say to tell you big-feller policeman come soon.'

Again Mr Wootton did not scoff.

'How does Canute know that?' he asked quietly. 'I was talking with Constable Pierce on the phone less than an hour ago, and he knew nothing about another policeman coming here. Canute's only guessing, Meena. Not worth a plug of tobacco.'

'Him and Murtee sit-down beside little fire last night,' Meena said seriously. 'Little fire. By themselves. The lubras not allowed to look.'

'But you did, eh?'

'I am not a lubra.'

'But you believe this silly magic?'

'Canute, Head Man. Murtee, Medicine Man.'

Wootton sensed the utter finality of this statement.

'I'll advance the tobacco, Meena. Tell Canute it will be a plug short next ration day. And tell Charlie and Rex to come back to work. Mustering to be done. They've been loafing around too long.'

Meena looked down at the seated man, encountering frankly his hard green eyes and sensing the powerful magnetism of the white man. She smiled as though because of his surrender, but knew there had been no surrender.

When in Loaders Springs next day, Wootton mentioned the tobacco incident to Constable Pierce, who seemed less sceptical than the cattleman, but agree it was a good tale to spin for a plug of tobacco.

However, the aborigines were right on the mark. At the third dawning following the announcement made by Canute per Meena, Detective Inspector Napoleon Bonaparte was seated against one of the pine trees overlooking the Mount Eden homestead, and down in the house yards was a riding hack and pack-horse which had brought him from the south two hours previously.

The stars were fading, and from the abyss below the ridge appeared a pavement of molten lead. Then it was as though lead ran in streams and rivers, was poured into bar-moulds, and soon all these isolated sheets of metal fused into a great plain of lead, spreading to the east, the north, and the south, until the vast slate supported the dome of the greening sky. When fan-tails of light further illuminated the sky, the sheen of the leaden expanse beneath faded, cold, ugly, inert.

There before Napoleon Bonaparte was The-Sea-That-Was; its headlands and its bays and its inlets, the coast stretching to the south and to the north, its level, silent surface of mud destitute of vegetation all the way to the far horizon, and farther still. Lake Eyre! The last puddle, sometimes to be filled with river water from the north, of The-Sea-That-Was, a puddle sixty miles wide and a hundred long.

Down in the viscous mud lie the bones of monstrous reptiles and animals, and man-catching birds. Along the curving shores, buried by drifting sand, are the mounds of shell fish gathered by the ancestors of Canute's tribe for feasts that kept them fat for generations.

What is geographically named 'the Lake Eyre Basin' roughly comprises two hundred thousand square miles, and most of it is below sea level. Save along the western edge, where run the rare trains northward to Alice Springs, the white population is less than two hundred, and the aborigines number but a hundred more. The rivers, when they run every decade or so, run uphill. Sand dunes float in the air and kangaroos leap from cloud to cloud. The horizon is never where it ought to be. A tree one moment is a shrub, and the next a radio mast. A reptilian monster sunning itself on a mountain ridge is, after all, a frilled lizard sprawled on the dead branch of a tree partially buried in a sand dune.

In this deceitful land a man and a child had vanished.

That had been an Everest of a problem for Senior Constable Pierce, and Bony, who came five weeks later, had to concede much to the policeman's reputation as a bushman and to all those many white men who had joined in the search. A deceitful land, yet it would not deceive any one of them to whom an area of two hundred thousand square miles would be on a par with a square mile of city blocks to the city dweller.

A man must eat, and during the hot summer months could not live a day without water. He dare not move a mile from water without carrying a supply, and water sources, other than the bores and at homesteads, were few indeed, after eleven rainless months. Every remaining supply had been watched by men whose eyes wouldn't fail to register the tracks of wild dogs, aborigines, cattle, and, if unable to decipher smoke signals, would note the whereabouts of aborigines, either in their wild state or semi-civilized. Were Ole Fren Yorky still alive, and there was no expressed doubt that he was, he had achieved remarkable success in eluding the finest desert men on earth.

They had been the prospectors trying to locate a man and a child. Now that Bony was arrived, he was, perforce, the mining engineer who would have to delve beneath the surfaces of this deceitful land.

So that when he came to Mount Eden after all prospecting had been done, he didn't fork a horse and race it here and there, or board a jeep and add to the normal dust, because it was apparently assumed that Yorky and the child were not lost, and, because of Yorky's bush experience, were not dead of thirst. Therefore, lives and planes hadn't been risked.

There were facts that could not be denied, and facts that could be assumptions, and assumptions that could be facts. A woman had been shot with a .44 rifle, and her daughter had been abducted from the homestead. A man seen near the homestead on the morning of the crime had left tracks within a few yards of the position of the body. When last seen, he had been carrying a .44 Winchester rifle.

The weekly windstorm raged that day, and those few tracks were sheltered from the wind by the homestead buildings. The man, with the child, had gained a lead over the searchers of some twenty hours, and over D.I. Bonaparte, five weeks.

Not a man had seen them since that day. Not one searcher had found a track left by either man or child, no tell-tale fire site, no sign of them whatsoever. Facts were few, assumptions many. One was that Yorky hadn't shot the mother and abducted the child, but that one of the five white men had returned that day, had shot the woman, with Yorky as witness, and the child also. Then had taken Yorky and the child to a distant place, and buried the bodies at the front of a moving sand dune, so placing the full responsibility on Ole Fren Yorky.

The all-seeing eagles knew the answer, as did the crows. The eagles this early morning came low to espy the stranger seated under the green tops of the pine trees, and the crows were equally interested, but quickly gave up when knowing he was alive. They indulged in insatiable curiosity in the stranger's horses down in the yards, and in two women who were trudging towards the house from the direction of the aborigines' camp. Some of the crows flew out a little way over Lake Eyre, and returned as though fearful, while several others continued on over the lake until Bony wondered if they intended to cross to the hidden shore beyond.

When smoke issued from a house chimney, Detective Inspector Bonaparte walked from the ridge down to the homestead of Mount Eden.

FOUR

MOUNT EDEN WELCOMES BONY

OF ALL Canute's subjects, numbering forty-three, only Sarah had not the slightest fear of him, and what fear, engendered by inherited instincts, she had of Murtee the Medicine Man was rarely manifest. She was one-fifth white, and four-fifths black, and all that her father contributed was a softening of the aboriginal lines of her features, and an acute sense of humour. It is told that before Canute was blinded by a grass fire, she laughed at him when in a towering rage, and that when Canute rushed at her, brandishing a waddy, she took it from him and knocked him cold, then stood over him and hugged herself tightly while laughing down at the silent one. It is also told of Sarah that in punishment Canute put the ban of silence on her, and she kicked him in the stomach and laughed right heartily.

Now that Sarah was cooking at 'government house', she and Meena rose early and arrived at the kitchen near enough to six every morning. It was her job first to prepare the morning tea which Meena took to Mr Wootton, whom she would surely find seated at the transceiver and talking with a neighbour.

This morning the fire had been lit and the water was simmering in the wide-bottomed kettle, and Meena was busily tidying the living-room, when there stepped into the kitchen one Sarah had never seen. She noted his lean dark face, the deep blue eyes, the white teeth, and the smile, the clean white shirt tucked into brown gabardine slacks. She said:

'No feller 'lowed here. What you want? Brekus not ready yet.'

'*I* am allowed here,' he told her, adding as though an afterthought, '*I* am allowed anywhere. Have you made morning tea yet?'

Without invitation he seated himself at the scrubbed table,

stretched his legs, smiled again at Sarah, who was undecided whether to be pleased or angry. It was the blue eyes which brought the indecision, they and the voice more than hinting at authority. Meena appeared, paused in the doorway to the living-room. Sarah swayed the teapot violently to assist the brewing, and, with the pot held by the handle and the tip of the spout, she asked:

'You big-feller policeman, eh?'

'Yes. You knew I was coming?'

Sarah nodded, placed the pot on the side of the stove, took cups and saucers from the dresser. The boss was forgotten. First she served the stranger. Standing before the visitor, Meena came to stand beside her, and Bony said:

'You are Sarah. And you are Meena. I shall be here some time. Is Mr Wootton up and about?'

'He's inside waiting for his tea,' replied Meena, recalling Sarah to her duties. 'What's your name?'

'Napoleon Bonaparte. If we ever become friends you may call me Bony. Meanwhile, please tell Mr Wootton that Inspector Bonaparte is here.'

'Inspector Bonaparte,' she repeated, and giggled. She cupped her hand about her breast, thrust forward her tummy, and again giggled. Sarah looked at her and dug an elbow hard into the ribs, which cut the giggle. She gasped, and managed to say: 'I thought you would be old, have grey hair, look fierce. You married?'

'Mr Wootton ... tell him I am here,' Bony urged gravely.

White or black, it makes no difference. Meena smiled at him, her hips swaying as she walked to the living-room. Once she looked back at him, and Sarah exclaimed:

'That Meena!' But there was pride and affection on her broad face.

Meena returned and nodded for Bony to enter the living-room, and, passing her, he tilted her chin and said:

'You will not be so saucy when I leave Mount Eden.'

The cattleman was standing with a tea-cup in one hand and a biscuit in the other. His expression was one of incredulity. His hair was tossed, and his moustache needed clipping.

26

'Inspector Bonaparte?' he questioned, with emphasis on the rank. 'Of what?'

'Of detectives, Mr Wootton,' suavely replied Bony. 'It seems that I am famous in some quarters and not so in others.'

'But we know nothing about you. The policeman at Loaders Springs knows nothing.'

'I asked him to know nothing,' calmly announced Bony. 'In fact I am ten days late, having been delayed on a case at Boulia.'

'In southwest Queensland? You came here by . . .?'

'Horse. I needed to meditate between murders, Mr Wootton. My credentials.'

Wootton placed cup and biscuit on the table and leaned forward to examine the open wallet, and the copy of the letter instructing Bonaparte to investigate the murder of Mrs Bell, for and on behalf of the South Australian Police department. Frowning, the cattleman straightened and stared into the blue eyes, so predominant in the dark face. He said:

'You have no objection to my contacting Senior Constable Pierce?'

'None whatever. By the way, your cook gave me a cup of tea which I left on her kitchen table. May I?'

'Meena!' called Mr Wootton. 'Bring Inspector Bonaparte another cup of tea and biscuits.'

Meena came in with the tea. Bony's eyes were directed to the polished panel of the transceiver, and her employer was at the wall telephone. Her gay mood had given place to one of curious watchfulness, and for a second or two she gazed at the slim figure with the squared shoulders, the straight back, before withdrawing with a rustle of her starched apron.

Bony was looking over the titles of the books, of which there must have been a hundred on the shelves beside the transceiver, when Wootton said:

'Pierce said he expected you. He said, also, that he told no one of your coming, in accordance with your instructions. And yet the blacks knew. The maid told me three days ago that a high-ranking policeman was coming. Doesn't add up, does it?'

'Oh yes, it adds up,' countered Bony. 'They communicate,

you know. Smoke signals, telepathy. I've been associated with them on the Boulia case.'

'On the killing of that aboriginal stockman? I've heard about it. You found the killer?'

'Of course.'

'Otherwise you would not be here now?'

'Naturally. I locate a killer once I start on his tracks.'

'I am afraid you won't get on the tracks of our murderer, Inspector. The wind wiped them out, bar at two places, and that a month back.'

'I was speaking metaphorically.'

'Oh! Well, anything I can do, we can all do, to help, you can be assured. . . . What d'you suggest?'

'I am in possession of the frame of this Mount Eden crime, and have to resurrect the flesh. That will take some time, in view of the reputation of Constable Pierce, and the thoroughness of his efforts. As you ask me to make suggestions—a room, a shower, breakfast.'

'Of course. Meena! I'll have the room prepared for you. Your things . . . where?'

'On the pack-horse I left in your horse yard.'

'Good! Meena! Call Charlie to fetch Inspector Bonaparte's gear from the pack-horse in the yard. And see to it that the corner room is ready for the Inspector. Tell Sarah about the extra breakfast. And, Meena, don't dally with Charlie.'

Meena smiled faintly and departed. She was both impressed and subdued.

'Pardon me remarking on it, Inspector, but your arrival indicates very early travelling.'

'It surely does, Mr Wootton. I came down the Birdsville Track on the mail truck to Maree, caught "The Ghan" to Coward Springs, where I contacted Constable Pierce and borrowed the horses. I made north and looked over the country southward of Lake Eyre. When day broke this morning I was meditating on the long ago of the aborigines. Always I have been interested in anthropology.'

'Sometimes I wish I had studied the subject,' Wootton said. 'You know, I've been here only five years, and it's my first experience of the country and the blacks. They defeat me. I hope some day to defeat the country.'

'You never will. No man ever has. But I know what you mean. Could you spare your men for the day?'

'Yes. I had work set for them, but it can wait.'

'Thank you. After breakfast, could we have them gathered somewhere that I may talk to them?'

'Of course. My office is large enough.'

'Kind of you. I will try not to inconvenience you more than necessary. This part of the Eyre Basin needs rain. When was the last rain?'

'Five months back. We want rain all right, but the ground feed is holding out. See anything of the floods up in Queensland?'

Bony could add nothing to Wootton's knowledge received over the radio, excepting to add his opinion that the water might reach Lake Eyre via Coopers Creek and possibly down the Warburton River. The cattleman sensed the determined avoidance of the subject in both their minds, and escorted Bony to the guest room.

At breakfast Bony raised the subject of Yorky's singular title.

'Oh, that!' Wootton said, chuckling. 'It happened years ago, before my time, anyway. I think Yorky is known, by repute, all over the back country. He's quite a character, or was before his mind must have become unhinged. No horseman, and useless as a stockman, but handy to have in dry times managing a pumping station, or riding a boundary fence.

'Like most of his type, he'd stick to a job for months, then suddenly leave with his cheque and make for a town. After drinking a cheque at Loaders Springs at the time I'm talking about, Yorky humped his swag out this way, intending to ask my predecessor for a job. The next thing was that the policeman at Loaders Springs – not Pierce, of course – rang through to say he'd received a report that Yorky was living with the blacks down on the creek, and would the owner of this place go along and bring him out. You know how it is, the law against a white man living in an aborigines' camp.

'Anyway, the cattleman, name of Murphy, rode to the camp. There was no one about excepting Chief Canute and a few of the lubras, including Sarah, now cooking for us. Sarah being more civilized than the rest, he called her and she came out of her humpy. Murphy said: "They tell me you got a white man in camp, Sarah. Tell him to come out at once." Sarah denied she had a white man in the camp, but Murphy persisted, until Sarah said: "No white feller in my camp, Boss. Only my ole fren Yorky." It appeared that Yorky turned up suffering badly from the booze, and Sarah took him in and was nursing him with soups and things.'

'Hence the Ole Fren Yorky,' supplemented the amused Bony. 'How old would he be, d'you think?'

'Difficult even to guess,' replied Wootton. 'I'd say in his early sixties.'

'Did you employ him ever?'

'Oh yes. He left here with his last cheque three weeks before he shot Mrs Bell. He'd been on another bender then, you see, when I found him at the blacks' camp. There were no aborigines there then. They were all away on walk-about.'

'Tell me about finding Yorky there.'

'Well, you see, it's my custom to go to Loaders Springs every week, and always on a Thursday. On that particular Thursday, I left about half past nine, per car. Half a mile along the track there's a gate, and just under another half mile there's a creek. The creek's always dry except after heavy rain, but between the road dip and the creek mouth with the Lake there's almost a permanent waterhole. They tell me the blacks have made it their headquarters for generations. Murphy let them fence it in from the cattle, and I've never interfered with them or the water.

'Well, that morning when I got there, I saw Yorky squatting over a bit of fire and drinking tea from a jam tin. I wondered why he'd camped there, when he had only to tramp another three-quarters of a mile to get here, and stopped to speak to him. He said he was sick, and he certainly looked it. He'd hoped the blacks would be there so's Sarah could look after him. And he pleaded for a drink – just a small reviver.

'I had a bottle of whisky in the car, and I gave him a hefty nobbler and told him to get along to the homestead and ask Mrs Bell to give him a feed. He said he would, and I drove on. A minute later, when I looked into the rear-vision mirror, I saw him on the track, swag up, even his rifle strapped to the swag.'

Bony pushed his empty plate a little from him, and drew closer the second cup of coffee.

'How did he appear to you . . . mentally?'

'All right, I think,' replied Wootton. 'Of course he was shaking a little, having been on the spirits for three solid weeks. The nobbler I gave him certainly bucked him up but no one will ever make me believe that drop of whisky drove him off his rocker enough to shoot Mrs Bell and clear out with the child. It's something I don't understand.'

'We shall,' Bony said, and rolled a cigarette.

FIVE

DIGGING

THE FOUR hands were invited into the office, Charlie and another aborigine being told they could take the day off. All four were familiar with the interior of this large room, and so noted that on the wall behind the desk had been tacked a large-scale map of Mount Eden.

Wootton occupied the chair behind the desk. Bony stood beside the desk, almost lazily smoking, while the four men sat and made themselves comfortable, at the invitation of their employer. Finally, obviously wondering what this was all about, they regarded Bony with deep interest.

'As you know, it is now several weeks since Mrs Bell was killed and her daughter abducted,' he began. 'Five weeks ago a man and a small child vanished, and both man and child were known to you better by far than I am known to you.

'Since that tragic day, you and many others were engaged in an intensive search for Ole Fren Yorky. You know the details of that search, and the balance of human effort within the extent of the country about Lake Eyre. No doubt you have assessed the chances of locating two human beings on an area of country many people outside would think to be a limitless world, in which fifty, a hundred, men could easily be lost. Thus you will agree with me that, despite all the hunting, all the planning, the chances of Yorky getting away, or holing up somewhere, were good from the beginning. The hunters held four kings, but Yorky held four aces. Correct?'

'Could be, and could not be,' doubted Arnold Bray. 'I don't reckon Yorky planned it. He was too sozzled to plan much. I said, and I still think, that the blacks helped him.'

'Knowing that Yorky was fairly close to the aborigines,' Bony proceeded to argue, 'knowing that all the aborigines were camped on the Neales River, the first thing Constable Pierce did was to send riders at top speed to cut off that line of retreat for Yorky. When the trucks for the trackers arrived at the Neales River, they made sure that every aborigine was there. As you say, Arnold Bray, Yorky never planned the murder. It was committed on impulse.'

'And then he was lucky enough to find he held four aces,' interrupted withered William Harte. 'In the first place, Yorky knows this country better than any of us, and, better than us, he can think closer to the abos. Put yourself in his place. . . . He done a murder before he even thought about it. He knows we're all away, that no one ain't likely to come around till middle afternoon. He's shot Mrs Bell, and he can't shoot the kid 'cos the reason he shot the woman ain't strong enough for him to shoot the kid. So he's got the kid on his hands 'cos the kid seen him doin' the shootin'. He's like a bloke having to walk with one boot on and the other off. So he looks over his cards, and decides he holds better cards than anyone else.'

Seated on the floor with his back to the wall, Harte paused to roll a cigarette, and Bony prompted him, the others apparently conceding his superior knowledge and experience.

'When he shot Mrs Bell,' resumed the ageless man, 'Yorky knew the country was wide open to him. He knew just where all the abos were . . . fifty miles something up north. He knows them abos pretty well, knows how their minds work, and the reason why he didn't shoot the kid was stronger than the reason why he ought to have shot her, to give him the best chance of getting clear out of this country. As I said, he knows the blacks better than any of us. He knows that once they're put to his tracks, even if them tracks is bits of dust in the air, they'll catch up with him. If they wants to, that is. He knows that if he kills the kid they'll want to; if he don't, they won't. That was his cards.'

'The aborigines thought much of Linda?' pressed Bony.

'They surely did. Like everyone else. One time we was playin' poker over in the quarters, and I drew a Queen of Hearts and snaffled the jackpot, and I said without thinking: "That's my Linda for you, fellers. The Queen of Hearts."

And that's what she was around these parts.'

'The aborigines, however, did try to track Yorky,' Wootton reminded him, and Bony was delighted at the course his conference was taking.

'Too right,' agreed Harte, who then had to go to the doorway for another spit. 'What happened? They're up on the Neales, half-starved, livin' on goannas and flies. They get brought back, and they're given lashings of beef and flour and tobacco to start 'em off right. Instead of huntin' a perenti or another feller's gin, they're set to huntin' Yorky.

'But do they hunt for Yorky? I got me doubts, and I got 'em because they knew he got aces. "Good ole Yorky," they'd say. "We'll look around, sort of, and feed up on the boss's beef, an' smoke the boss's baccy." But they didn't just look around, as you said, Mr Wootton. They set to work all right, but not because they hate Yorky for killing Mrs Bell. They set to work like bloodhounds to make sure Yorky hadn't killed Linda and planted her body somewhere, and when they reasoned that Yorky hadn't been that ruddy stupid, that he'd got clear away with the kid, they sort of got tired and gradually eased up till they quit. That's why I say Ole Fren Yorky knew when he collared Linda that he held all the aces.'

'And he will continue to hold them while he keeps Linda Bell alive?' encouraged Bony.

'That's so. While he's got Linda with him, it's Yorky's game.'

'And you still don't think that the blacks know where he is?' drawled lanky Eric Maundy.

'No, I don't think they do, Eric. To find that out would mean work, and they'd be satisfied to know that little Linda was safe enough. They'd say Yorky and the kid was around somewhere, that Yorky would come out of smoke when it suited him, and meanwhile Charlie will be chasing Meena, and Canute will scratch his neck 'cos he's too old to take her even though she was promised to him when she was born. You gotta know them abos, Eric.'

'Reckon you know 'em?' jibed the young man named Harry Lawton.

'If you think you know 'em better, put up a better yarn,' advised Arnold with asperity.

'If we accept your idea,' Bony contributed, 'where is Yorky obtaining food for himself and the child?'

'At his camps,' replied Harte. 'Perhaps you don't know that when Yorky left here for a bender, he had a job riding the boundary fence.'

'That's so,' added Wootton. 'The boundary fence is some hundred and fifty miles round the station, bar where it cuts into the Lake. Yorky rode it with camels. He had a camp every twenty miles, with water at every second camp.'

'And them camps were stocked with tucker,' inserted Harte. 'You know, flour and tea and sugar kept in tins and tinned dog and fish if he was stuck. I asked him once about the abos getting down on his tucker and tobacco, and he laughed and said they wouldn't steal from him.'

Bony studied the wall map of Mount Eden Station. To Wootton he said:

'Mark the camps, please, and mark additionally those camps where the water is.' To Harte he said: 'What's outside the boundary fence?'

'Nothing. Open country, excepting down south and south-east.'

'Wild aborigines?'

Harte shook his head, saying:

'Not till you get up about the Simpson Desert, and they ain't as wild as they used to be.'

'The country . . . dry all the way up north and west?'

'Same as around here. Haven't had no rain for months, and that fell at the wrong time. Still, there's water if you know where to find it. Water holes up on the Neales. Water under the Lake mud, if you can stomach it.'

'H'm! We seem to be going somewhere.' Bony looked at each in turn. 'I want you to mark on this map where each of you went that day Mrs Bell was shot, and note also the time when you were farthest from the homestead. That is, as close as possible. A blue pencil, Mr Wootton, please.'

They did as requested. Then Bony said:

'I understand that you four men have been in this part of Australia for many years, much longer than Mr Wootton. You have been most co-operative, and I ask you to continue so. It is good to know that you believe Linda is still alive, and that rescuing her must take priority. I would not have expected such full co-operation, were it not for the possibility of recovering the child.

'You will see clearly that the actual rescue could well be attended by grave danger to her from the man who abducted her. To save himself he might kill her. It is of vital importance to know exactly the kind of man he is, or was, before he shot Mrs Bell. First, let us try to understand why he shot Mrs Bell. Had he ever expressed dislike of her?'

'Not that I ever heard,' replied Arnold. 'He was one of them inoffensive poor bastards. Never hardly spoke unless spoken to. You had to get him alone, and sort of talk soft to him, before he'd open up. He'd talk fast enough to Linda, and the black kids.'

'When drunk or recovering from a bout, did he think of women, talk about them?'

'No.'

'Did Mrs Bell ever express dislike of him, ever strongly criticise him?'

'Just the opposite. Mrs Bell sort of liked him, I think. Patched his shirts more than once.'

'After he'd washed 'em,' chuckled young Harry Lawton. 'She'd do that for any of us.'

'You're too flash to have old shirts to be patched,' drawled Eric.

'She never objected to Linda talking to Yorky?'

'Don't think. Had no reason to. He was harmless enough.'

'Yorky must have gone wonky to have shot her,' insisted Eric.

'All right! Then let us get down to his association with the aborigines,' pressed Bony. 'You have said he was close to them. In what way? Did he live secretly with a lubra?'

Harry Lawton broke into laughter, and was silenced by the glare in Arnold's grey eyes. It was Harte who replied.

36

'Look, Inspector. Yorky was older than me. Not much, but still he was so. I remember Yorky coming into this country about thirty-five years back. Not much to look at but real rough: always small and a bit wispy, if you know what I mean. And I can't say he'd had much education, less, sort of, than Meena and Charlie and the other abos who went down to Mission School for a spell.

'Yorky could read the papers, follow the races and all that. But he got to know more about the ants and things than ever I wanted to, and he got to know the ways of camels when he was frightened of horses. I don't think he was more taken up with women than most of us. Camped for a night or two with one down at Loaders Springs. You know the sort. Some say that there was times when he camped with Sarah, and I have heard that there was times when he had a young lubra with him on the boundary fence. A long time ago, though.'

Harte went again to the door to spit.

'But this is what I am trying to get out. Yorky was more interested in watching ants and birds than he was in talking about cattle and horses like the rest of us. He'd get the black kids to take him out and show him things. All the kids took to him, and they run like hell from me. Gradually he got in with the blacks. And I'm sure it wasn't to get at the lubras. He was sort of interested in them like he was in the ants. He'd give them things. Fork out tobacco, buy a dress or some such.'

'I once told him he oughta write a book about 'em,' interrupted Harry Lawton. 'He knows more about 'em than the perfessors and them sort of blokes.'

'He could have done, too, if he'd had any education,' agreed Harte. 'Well, that's how it is with Ole Fren Yorky. You heard how he got the name?'

'Yes. And what you have said supports what I already know of him,' replied Bony, and bending over the desk he jotted a note on a slip of paper. 'It does seem that Yorky must have lost his balance through the booze to have shot Mrs Bell. Could you say he tended to be mentally childish?'

'No,' said Arnold with conviction. 'Yet he wasn't . . . I don't know how to put it. He reminds me of a nephew of mine down in Adelaide. Used to moon about when other kids were playing or larking. Got so when he grew older that he went around dreaming. But he had brains. Ended by being a first class commercial artist with a publishing firm in Sydney. No, Yorky was never wonky. The way he plays poker proves that.'

'He had what I'd call low cunning,' commented Lawton. 'You could never tell what cards he held.'

'So that all of you actually find it hard to believe that Ole Fren Yorky did shoot Mrs Bell?' asked Bony.

'That's about it,' agreed Arnold, and the others nodded agreement. 'There's times when I won't belive it.'

'You are sure those were his tracks you picked out?'

'Too right! Couldn't mistake 'em,' replied Harte.

Bony presented his note to Arnold, and said:

'When I locate Yorky, we shall know all about it. The motive will be interesting; the way of his escape will be interesting too.'

Arnold nodded to Harte, and they left the office. The others watched them leave, knowing they did so at the behest of Bony's note. Wootton cleared his throat preparatory to saying something, and was stopped by a screech from without.

Struggling figures appeared in the doorway, and the men brought in a furious lubra.

SIX

THE ART OF REASONING

'LEMME GO, you Arnold Bray. Lemme go, I say,' shouted Sarah, and, having inserted the large woman into the office, Arnold and Harte freed her arms and blocked the doorway. Either Sarah was in excellent form, or the struggle hadn't lasted long, but she now stood with fists balled into her hips, a glare in her eyes, and requiring only a broomstick or a rolling-pin to ape her white counterpart.

'She was round at the back wall with her ear to a crack,' announced Arnold. 'Just listening in.'

'I was only sittin' in the shade outside that hot ole kitchen,' shouted Sarah, and Wootton would have spoken had not Bony said, placatingly:

'Well, there's no harm in that, Sarah. It's deep shade here, and you are entitled to it. Still, there's house shade outside the kitchen door, and I saw only an hour ago a nice chair. You go there and sit in that easy chair, or even better, what about morning tea?' Again Wootton attempted to speak, but Bony waved him to silence. The lubra's black eyes encountered the blue eyes of the slim Napoleon Bonaparte, blue eyes hinting at laughter, friendliness, and abruptly she smiled:

'Mornin' tea! Crikey! I forgot about it. That Meena! She should of told me.'

Nodding to Bony, she turned about, scowled at the men and went out like a cork down a drain.

'Well, what d'you make of that?' demanded Wootton, his face flushed. 'Eavesdropping for sure. You should have made her tell us why she was doing that, Inspector!'

'You cannot make those people do anything they don't wish to do,' Bony said, coldly. 'That she was listening is a point, but only that. We have to remember that she and Yorky were friends, and that she must be interested in his fate, as we are. I think you men may leave. Perhaps this afternoon or this evening we could get together again and talk. All right with you?'

They assented: then as they were about to go, young Lawton asked:

'Mind telling why you wanted us to mark that map with where we were that day Mrs Bell was murdered?'

'Not at all. It was mere police routine. You see, any one of you four men could have returned after Mr Wootton left that day, then shot Mrs Bell and taken the child away and killed her. Even you, Mr Wootton, could have done just that.'

'But what about Yorky? Yorky was known to come here that morning,' pressed Lawton, and the others nodded quick agreement.

'As I told you, it is merely police routine to establish the whereabouts of everyone at the assumed time the crime was committed. In fact I think Constable Pierce asked for that information, and that it is recorded in his report.'

'He did make a song and dance about it,' admitted young Lawton. 'Looks like we're all sort of suspect, don't it?'

'Pierce acted rightly,' patiently continued Bony. 'Look at it this way. Not one of you is supported by a witness as to what you did between the time you left the homestead and the time you returned. No one saw Yorky at the blacks' camp other than Mr Wootton. To be sure, Bill Harte found Yorky's tracks back of the meat-house, and showed them to Arnold Bray, who agreed they were his. To be sure, Yorky's tracks were found at the homestead gate. Pierce took plaster casts of those tracks. Before Yorky is put on trial, if he is, the casts must prove that he actually made those tracks, that he was, in fact, at this homestead on that morning. A good policeman, and Pierce is a good policeman, leaves nothing to chance.'

'Fair enough,' supported Wootton. 'All right, you men can take the day off, and if you think of anything, I'm sure the Inspector will be happy to talk it over.'

They were drifting across the square to the quarters when the morning tea gong was beaten, and they about-turned and went back to the meal annexe. Tea and buttered scones were served by Meena to Bony and his host on the house veranda, and when she had withdrawn, Bony questioned about her.

He learned that a religious body conducted a Mission Church and school a few miles out from Loaders Springs. Aborigines, both adults and children, were warmly welcomed. A large number of children chose to live at the Mission, chose to because there was no compulsion. They were taught the elementary subjects – drawing and painting, basketwork, needlework, woodwork, and in return assisted the pastor and his wife with the stock and the garden.

'I visited the place one afternoon,' Wootton said. 'Surprised me, the work the children were doing in class. And how they sang, too! I had only just come here, was still raw to the country, and I asked the pastor what happened to the children when they left. He said: "Oh, the lads become stockmen, and the girls do domestic service round about. That's when it suits them. We do our best, as we hope you can see, but after they leave us, the old ones get them back." '

'I can understand that,' Bony agreed with the pastor. 'Meena, though, seems to be an excellent maid.'

'I think so. Yes, she's good in a house. But then neither she nor Sarah will stay here overnight, and there's no telling that they'll turn up in the morning, or go off with the others on a walkabout. That girl can sew and mend as good as Mrs Bell could. And Charlie – you saw him this morning – is a damn fine wood carver.'

Wootton stretched his thin, short legs and lit his pipe.

'You ought to see the dolls he carved for little Linda Bell. One is the dead spit of Ole Fren Yorky, and there's another you'd say was my image. The one supposed to be Mrs Bell isn't so good, but another one, of Meena, to my mind, is the best of the lot. We'll go and see them if you like. They're over in the playhouse.'

'Yes, I'd like to see them. I understand that the men built the playhouse. Which reminds me: did Linda spend much of her days there?'

'A good deal, Inspector,' replied the cattleman reflectively.

'You know, you can't wonder that we worshipped that child. Every Sunday afternoon she'd invite us all there for tea. Had her own tea set and her mother filled the teapot. I went sometimes. She'd have her visitors squatting on the floor, and she'd hand down her small cups and saucers and plates of scones and cake; and the men would talk to her with exaggerated politeness, and she would be the little lady.' Wootton sighed. 'Only that last day I was commissioned to buy a box of chocolates and special handkerchiefs for her.'

A few minutes later they left the house for the canegrass playhouse. It was noticeable how the thick walls shut out the noises of the crows, the windmill raising water, and the soft hissing of the gusty wind over the ground. Standing within the entrance, Bony surveyed the interior, noting the cut-down furniture, and the fact that objects were not positioned as described by Constable Pierce. Almost at once Wootton exclaimed:

'Why, two of the dolls have gone! They were set up on the shelf bench. And those presents. The comb and the box of handkerchiefs have gone too. Now, what the hell!'

'When did you last see them?' asked Bony.

'Oh, about a fortnight back. The men wanted to tidy up the place, having the idea of making it nice for Linda's return. I obtained permission from Pierce, and they went to work. Swept the floor, cleaned the window, put the dolls side by side on the bench, and the presents on the bench, too. I'll call them.'

Bony heard Wootton shouting. He surveyed this room, and was saddened by its emptiness of personality. The cut-down table and chair, the books, the old trunk, and small dresser with the bright chintz curtain only hinted at a life which once had warmed this place. Oddly enough, he felt himself to be an intruder.

They came crowding in, Wootton and his men, silently taking in this well-remembered place.

'Ole Fren Yorky and Meena gone off on walkabout all right,' exploded Harry Lawton.

'And the handkerchiefs, and the comb, the blue one,'

42

drawled Eric with fierce breathlessness. 'Left the chocolates. They was no good anyhow. Heat melted 'em.'

Harte quietly went forward and gazed along the surface of the shelf bench. His voice was cold.

'Who was in here last? I was looking in Sunday, week back, and them dolls was all there where we put 'em in a row. I remember how Meena was sort of turned to look at the boss. It wasn't yestiddy, nor the day before, they were took. There's plenty of dust fell on the places where they were sitting.'

They talked. They pondered. Finally they agreed that the last man to look into the playhouse had been Bill Harte and that had been nine days ago. All remembered that the dolls were then on the bench, and that the presents Linda was to have received that day her mother was shot were also set out on the bench.

'Them ruddy blacks have raided the place,' Harry Lawton accused.

'We'll find out right now,' decided Eric. 'Come on, let's argue it out with old Canute. He'll make the thief part up ... or else.'

Anger charged the quiet air, and then Bony spoke:

'I would like you to leave the matter to me, and to say nothing of it in the hearing of Sarah and Meena,' he said with easy authority. 'Now just see what else has been taken ... books, from that dresser, anything?'

Arnold examined the books, shook his head. He lifted the curtain in front of the dresser, disclosing a dainty tea service, a box containing coloured wools, and material. Again he shook his massive head and dropped the curtain. Eric cried:

'Wait on, Arnold! Them cups and things.'

He sprang forward and lifted the curtain. Then he straightened, paused to be supported on his discovery, finally shouted quite unnecessarily:

'There was six cups and saucers. Now there's only five. Look! A cup and saucer has been pinched, too.'

Men swore. Bony said:

'Keep on looking. Be sure if anything else is missing.'

Dolls to comfort a little girl. A china cup for her to drink

43

from instead of a tin mug, perhaps a jam tin. Handkerchiefs and blue comb taken, but not a box of chocolates spoiled by the heat.

Aboriginal children would not have ignored the chocolates, although ruined by heat.

'Her Kurdaitcha shoes,' drawled Bill Harte. 'They don't seem to be here, either.'

The Kurdaitcha Man of legend, the fabulous being who walks by night, his feet covered with emu feathers glued with blood so that he leaves no tracks for aborigines to follow when it is light. Harry Lawton withdrew from the search to tell Bony that Charlie had fashioned imitation shoes for Linda.

'Yes, those pretty pieces have gone, too,' Arnold declared. 'All decorated with feathers and pictures drawn on 'em with hot wire. Old Murtee could have taken them for his collection of magic things.'

Eventually it was agreed that nothing else had been removed. Eric again suggested 'arguing it out' with Canute, and it was Arnold who told him, 'That's out,' because Inspector Bonaparte said so. It was noticeable that their first reaction of cautious familiarity towards Bony was replaced by firming respect, for, as it had been with so many others in the past, his eyes, his voice and speech caused them to forget his mixed race. He was saying:

'It is often wise to set aside the act in favour of the motive. Just now when we found Sarah listening to us, the act might be of smaller importance than the reason prompting her. So it is with these missing articles belonging to Linda Bell. Who took them is of lesser interest to me than why they were taken. Assuming, of course, that they were not removed by the aboriginal children, or by someone intending to give them to the children.'

'I think I see your point, Inspector,' observed Wootton. 'Someone could have taken them to Linda, wherever she is with Ole Fren Yorky.'

'Proving that Linda is still alive,' added Arnold with satisfaction.

'That Linda wanted them things to play with,' hopefully supplemented Eric. 'Could of been that Yorky came here himself to get 'em.'

'We'd have seen his tracks,' Arnold said.

'Not if he came last Sat'day, or yesterday week,' objected Bill Harte. 'Them two days it blew like hell, and blew all night too, remember.'

'It could be more likely that one of the aborigines stole them to take them to Yorky for Linda,' contributed Wootton.

'So we come back to the abos,' crowed young Lawton.

'Yair, the abos, Harry,' agreed Eric. 'We'll get it out of them. Who pinched the dolls and things, and what was done with 'em. Now what-in-'ell you smiling about, Inspector?'

'I'm beginning to wonder who is the detective,' Bony replied. 'Inductive reasoning must keep to specified rules, and often to indulge in such reasoning is unwise until all the available facts and probable assumptions are marshalled. There is an assumption which has not yet occurred to you, an assumption which we have authority to examine. We may assume that the presents and the dolls were removed by someone with the intention of putting into our minds the idea that Linda is still alive. The motive for that is obscure, but still reasonable to accept.'

From Bony they looked at each other, bewilderment plainly evident. To make confusion stick, he went on:

'Recall what I said about the tracks you believed were left by Yorky. Until proved, we may only assume he made them, and we may assume someone else falsified them, knowing that most people see what they want to see. So there is one assumption we may add to another, and those two to yet a third, and then we have a faint glimmer of a theory.

'Crime investigators are trained minds. I have been trained to think along lines of deduction and induction. These are two separate processes of thinking, as doubtless you know. Or perhaps you don't know. Which is why I require you not to question the aborigines, or to mention this matter to the domestics over the way. Is that understood?'

Eric coughed and nodded. Young Harry nodded and looked

vacant. Arnold was thoughtful, and Bill Harte's bright dark eyes were curious. Mr Wootton blinked and spoke for all.

'I think we follow you, Inspector Bonaparte. You may depend on us not to interfere.'

'I was sure I could depend on you,' suavely returned Bony.

SEVEN

SAVAGES AND BYRON

THE FIRE was like the red and flickering eye of Ganba, the Great Snake. Tall white pillars encircled the fiery eye, and between these pillars the sweet notes of Ganba's snoring floated on to warn the aborigines in all Australia that he was out from his chambers under the earth.

The fire burned redly amid the white gums surrounding the waterhole. Ganba's snoring was coming from a length of hollow tree branch called a dijeridoo and played by an aborigine whose hair and beard were white, whose naked chest and back was cicatriced in fantastic designs and marks.

The audience of men stared into Ganba's red eye. Behind them sat their women, the young girls and the children. All the babies were either asleep or watching with large and rounded eyes. Only occasionally did one move, and then slightly, so engrossed were they by the voice of the dijeridoo.

The dijeridoo was as thick as a man's leg, and so long that the end rested on a sheet of bark beyond Canute's outstretched feet. The mouth end was but little smaller than the far opening, and from it issued sounds, which, to ears accustomed to white man's music, would be meaningless.

Canute was telling a story which was first told when Lake Eyre was part of a great sea.

There was a woman who lived in a cave on a hill, a wise woman who could see far and who heard the birds talking. With her was her son, a stripling, a beautiful youth. Now the day came when a party of the woman's people were to leave for a distant country to trade magic churinga stones for spear shafts. These men came to the woman and asked that her son might go with them, and so begin to become a man.

The woman consented, and the youth departed with the traders, and they were away for a long time, until the woman,

47

anxiously watching from her cave, saw them come over a ridge far away. Slowly and often she counted them, and the number was short by one.

The traders said that a great man-bird had swooped down upon them and taken the youth into the sky and given him to its fledglings in a nest on a pile of stones. They hid themselves in hollow trees and dared not come out till night came.

So, as custom dictated, all the men cut into themselves the mourning marks, and all the women cut their breasts and lamented for five days. On the sixth day the woman called the traders to sit before her cave. She spoke soft words to them, and gave them honey ants on palm leaves to eat, and sweet water in little gourds to drink. And one by one they fell over, and told her they had killed the beautiful youth because all the maidens rejoiced over him and would not look upon them.

They died, and the woman made a big fire and burned them, and she raised her arms to lift the sky high and permit a tall willi-willi to sweep over the world and kick the bones to dust.

Was it Canute telling this story? How can a story be told unless with words? You may say that music can tell a story for those with ears to hear, but you would be the last to say that Canute was producing music. Shall we compromise, agree that Canute was passing on the old old stories for those with ears to hear and minds to interpret them? For from that dijeridoo issued no tune, no rhythm, no note to be even imagined as musical.

Detective Inspector Napoleon Bonaparte listened raptly to the story of the woman and the beautiful youth. None was aware that he stood behind one of the white pillars.

A lean old man sat beside Canute. His arms rested on his knees, his face resting on the crossed arms. Bony saw Sarah, who was nursing a naked baby. Her face was lifted as though pictures were strung between two of the white gums. Meena was there, wearing a blue skirt, her body naked above the waist, the soft firelight shimmering like golden dew on her untapped breasts. Like many of the others, she was gazing into

48

the heart of the fire. The young man Bony knew as Charlie was there too, watching Meena.

Bony had listened to more than the outline of the story. He had heard the tramp of the willi-willi coming across the world, the clash and crash of pounded bones kicked to dust. He had seen the cave, the very stones of its entrance, the woman tall and graceful, and the stripling son as he walked down the hill to pass into the keeping of his murderers. Bony had felt the wind, heard it in the trees and in the grass. He had watched the lie swoop down from the sky, the lie which was a giant bird with a man's head. He had shrunk away from the evil of the bird's face, and he had thrilled as he watched the agony of the poisoned liars.

He was but half way from the white man toward these descendants of the ancient inhabitants. He heard, and saw the pictures, because he knew the story. Thus he could follow and interpret the sounds issuing from the dijeridoo. But when Canute told another story of which he was ignorant, the sounds were of no help, told him no story, but did create pictures of flat water, waving tobacco bush, wind stirring sand grains. The story was told and another begun, and he received pictures sometimes blurred, sometimes sharply clear, in rapid alternation.

He fancied, for it could have been nothing more than fancy, that he saw a white man heavily burdened. The load he carried was larger than himself. Later, he saw a white man crawling on hands and knees. The noises from the hollow instrument filed past his ears, each one isolated. It was as though one laughed as it passed, another cried, another whispered something he couldn't hear. He saw a man, a slim man. His hair was black and straight. His face was pale. He was groping to identify this man and did identify him when he was struggling to look, as through fog, upon a child whose skin was white, and then was black, and in whose arms snuggled a spirit baby created by mirage water.

Another picture commanded his mind, stayed there for a fraction of a second, fled into the darkness behind his closed eyes. The flash picture was of a ghost, a woman running from

49

him, and on her back a question mark.

And then he was following another remembered story, this time of two young aborigines who robbed the nest of an eagle and were captured by a dingo with an eagle's head, and who made them carry him because he had a burr in his foot.

The last note of a musical instrument is emphasized by the vacuum of silence, like the bottom of a well receiving a stone. When the sounds of the dijeridoo ceased, there was no silence, the minds of those listening continuing to hear what the ears no longer registered.

Bony could not be sure when the dijeridoo stopped, nor when he realized that it had done. On opening his eyes, he saw that Canute was rolling a cigarette, the dijeridoo was lying on the ground at his side, and the audience was still captive. He noted, too, that Meena was the first to be conscious of her surroundings, and immediately after her, a woman and a young man. Meena rose and soundlessly departed to the deeper shadow of a humpy before the others broke from the spell, and those closest in blood to the pure aborigine were the last to be released by Canute's 'art'.

Stepping round the trunk of the tree, Bony leaned against it and brought fingers to work making a cigarette. Someone tossed wood into Ganba's red eye, and the initiated men moved nearer to Canute and his chief henchman, Murtee. Then Bony struck a match and applied the flame to his cigarette.

Those about the fire turned at the sound, save the Medicine Man and the Chief. Bony went forward, ebony images now frozen, waiting inscrutably. He passed round a right flank of them, and seated himself crosslegged when the Elders were directly to his front. Dark eyes reflected the firelight, not unlike black opals.

Bony smoked his cigarette, and not a word was said, nor a gesture made. It was as though they occupied one side of a gulf and could be reached only by him who had wings to fly. Slowly, Bony made another cigarette, and casually smoked that to the last half-inch, and still no word was spoken.

All of them, and there were seventeen, were in excellent

50

physical condition, several being positively fat. Canute wore good cloth trousers and no shirt. Murtee wore a blue silk shirt, trousers and tennis shoes. Two were smoking good-quality pipes. Knowing he would have to attempt the flight, Bony spoke.

'You are Orrabunna men. I am Worcair man.'

He knew his assessment of the degree of their nearness to the whites was accurate when Canute said:

'My mother was emu totem and my father was jerboa. I am emu man.'

'My mother! I don't know her totem. My father was a white man. My other father is my brother and my son, my uncle and my grandfather. His name was Illawallie. He was head man of the Worcair. The marks of the Worcair are on me.'

Canute stood, saying:

'Let me know with my hands.'

Bony stood, removed his shirt, and the old man's fingers traced the cicatrices on his back and chest. Then his fingers traced his features, and finally his hands to each fingertip. That being done, Bony resumed his shirt and they sat.

'Long time ago you sealed to Worcair people. Now you white-feller policeman,' pronounced Canute. After a long silence he asked: 'What you want from Orrabunna men?'

'Two spirit people made by Charlie and given to Linda Bell.'

Canute again fell silent, and before Murtee spoke Bony knew that to the Medicine Man the buck had been passed.

Murtee stroked the thin grey beard falling from his lean face.

'Ole Fren Yorky and Meena have gone up to the sky. Mr Wootton and Missus Bell no good for sky. They make sky fall down.'

'Who took them from the playhouse along at homestead?'

'Kurdaitcha Man. I look into little fire and Kurdaitcha Man tell me. Kurdaitcha Man and spirit Meena and Ole Fren Yorky, all go up into sky?'

'Kurdaitcha Man, liar, eh!' charged Bony. 'Ole Fren Yorky go up into sky maybe, but Meena still here. What

51

for Kurdaitcha Man not take Meena up into sky, but take Spirit Meena up into sky?'

That was as far as he progressed. First Murtee and then Canute pushed him back over the gulf separating the two races, and began to treat him as a white visitor.

Murtee laughed as though amused. Canute chuckled mechanically. The other men smiled and joked among themselves. They wiggled their toes, bunched shoulders, scratched their arms. They occupied their side of the gulf, and Bony the side where stand the white men who actually believe the aborigines are ludicrous savages.

'What say you hand those dolls back to Mr Wootton to look after for Linda?' Bony suggested, and old Canute chuckled again and cheerfully denied any one of his people had taken them. Murtee shrugged, stroked his beard.

'Charlie's ole dolls not in this camp. The ole dolls belong to Linda. Perhaps some day Linda come back, then she want them,' observed Murtee, laughing, without the slightest cause to laugh. Canute almost rolled over, such was his spurious front, and the others copied his lead. Bony laughed with them, making them uneasy because unsure if his merriment was real or mockery. Their faces grew swiftly serious when he leaned forward to the fire and withdrew several burning sticks, which he placed with flaming ends together, to form a separate fire.

Before this small fire he squatted, and across his bunched knees he rested a forearm, and with a metal tobacco box he rubbed his forehead, as though it were a magic churinga stone, before sinking his face to the forearm. They became distinctly uneasy, for Bony's spirit might well be about to leave his body and talk with the Kurdaitcha Man up in the sky. Murtee whispered, and Canute thus followed the act. Referring to the Medicine Man living near Boulia where he had but recently been on investigation, Bony lifted his head, saying:

'Boulia feller, called Eruki, he been tell me he told you long time ago I was coming to Mount Eden. So you been talking to Eruki up in the sky. What say you now talk to Ole Fren Yorky and tell him to bring Linda Bell back to Mount Eden? All you blackfellers good fellers. You all been looking for tracks. Now you sit down and talk magic, like you talk magic to Eruki. You send your spirit, Canute, and your spirit, Murtee, up into sky to talk with Kurdaitcha Man. Tell him to come down and into Ole Fren Yorky and make him bring Linda back.'

They were again images, ebony images with opal flashing eyes. As he had confused five white men that morning, so now he left the black men equally confused. Rising to his feet, he stared down into each pair of flickering eyes, and then left the camp and passed into the wall of dark night.

If you cannot create a tree, plant a seed.

As soundlessly as he had approached the camp, he departed from it, and he had almost gained the road when a singular noise halted him. It was followed by another he could not tab, and, crouching to the ground to gain a skyline, he saw two figures under a low tree bordering the track. A man and a woman were facing each other. They were holding hands and swaying backward and forward like children playing.

Silhouetted against a dull screen, they were sharply etched nevertheless. The man freed the woman's hands and then thrust his hands forward, palms upward like cups. The cups touched the woman's breasts, and she lashed out and smacked the man's face. The man laughed, though the blow must have been painful, and then he sprang forward and clasped the woman, whose face was tilted to take his kisses.

Bony veered to the left, silently walked parallel with the track until he was sure his retreat was unobserved.

'Well, well, and well, well!' he breathed. 'Romantic Byron! Who listens once will listen twice; her heart be sure is not of ice, and one refusal no rebuff.'

EIGHT

MUCH ADO ABOUT A BLOODSTAIN

THE FOLLOWING morning when Meena waited at the breakfast table, she placed the food before Wootton and Bony efficiently and with no trace of either nervousness or servility. Her large dark eyes never once met those of the guest, however, and yet there was no apparent avoidance, no revelation of consciousness of the visit to her camp. When she had departed for the kitchen Wootton asked:

'What's your programme today?'

'Oh, I have to contact Pierce,' casually replied Bony. 'First, though, I would like to talk with William Harte before he leaves for the day's work. You won't mind?'

'Not at all.' Wootton brushed his moustache with his napkin. 'As I said yesterday, anything any of us can do. Did you inquire about the missing dolls at the blacks' camp last night?'

It was a natural question, Bony having been absent from the homestead, and in view of the talk in the playhouse about the dolls.

'Yes, I did,' he replied. 'I talked to Canute and his Medicine Man. Put it to them straight about the dolls. They both said they knew nothing, and were sure no one of their people had stolen them.'

'It must have been one of them, or one of us five white men,' argued Wootton. 'No one else has been around the place since Harte last saw the dolls on the bench. As someone said yesterday, Yorky could have come back for them, but that would have been rather risky for him, wouldn't it? Wouldn't the blacks have known?'

'Likely enough to both questions.'

'Then you think the blacks know where Yorky is hiding out?'

'Yes and no to that one, Mr Wootton.' Bony smiled disarmingly, adding, 'You have not been long enough in this country to know that to hasten is to crawl, and to crawl is to hasten.'

'But the child, Inspector.'

'Her condition will not be bettered or worsened at this point. Permit me to ask the questions. Tell me, Mrs Bell was shot on February 7th. Late that night the policeman and the doctor arrived. When was the body taken to Loaders Springs?'

'Next day. The doctor took it in his station wagon. She was buried at Loaders Springs.'

'Did he leave before or after the aborigines came in the trucks sent for them?'

'He left after lunch, and the trucks didn't return till after sundown. Why all this?'

'Now, now! I ask the questions. Charlie carved the dolls' heads and tinted the faces. Who made the clothes?'

The cattleman frowned, obviously uncertain.

'Couldn't rightly say. Mrs Bell, I think. Might have been Meena. Shall I call her?'

'Please do.'

Without rising, Wootton called, and the girl came, to stand placidly awaiting his orders.

'Meena, who made the clothes for Mr Wootton, Mrs Bell, and Ole Fren Yorky?'

'I did.'

'All of them?'

They could see that Meena was wriggling her toes in her red shoes, although to them her feet were not visible. She giggled, and the small white teeth momentarily pressed down on the lower lip. In that moment she was remarkably attractive. She said:

'I didn't make Mr Wootton's trousers, or Ole Fren Yorky's. The ones I made, Linda didn't like because she couldn't take 'em off. So Mrs Bell made new ones that Linda could take off and put on.'

'And what happened to the trousers you made?' asked Bony.

'I don't know what Linda did with them.'

'Who stuffed the dolls' bodies?'

'Mrs Bell tried hard.' Again Meena giggled – a delightful sound. 'I did first. Then Linda tried. Then Mrs Bell had a go. Arnold did it in the end with sawdust in the carpenter's shop.'

'And Charlie carved the heads, painted them, and put the hair and whiskers on the men?'

Meena's eyes rested steadily on Bony, who could then see the grey flecks in the dark irises. She nodded, and Bony buttered a piece of toast.

'Did he carve them when supposed to be working for Mr Wootton?'

'No. No time for anything when station work going on. He did them any old time.'

'How much was he paid for them?'

This question brought a change of expression. Indignation gleamed in the dark eyes, shadowed the voice.

'Nothing at all. Charlie work for nothing . . . for Meena.'

'Did them for nothing!' echoed Bony, and now the honey skin darkened, and once again came the joyous giggle.

'Well, I paid Charlie,' she said. 'I give him one kiss for Mr Wootton, one for Mrs Bell, and one for Ole Fren Yorky. Not till he done them and give them to Linda.'

'Oh! And how many kisses did you pay for Meena?'

'Why you want to know? But I'll tell. I'm not scared. I let him kiss me twice for Meena, 'cos he worked double as hard on her.'

'When are you going to marry that feller?' asked Wootton and Bony was surprised by the firmness in his voice.

'I belong to old Canute,' replied Meena, swift rebellion in her eyes and voice.

'Rubbish! Young woman like you unclaimed because of that stupid old custom.'

It was a pity that Wootton said that, because it banished the girl's natural frankness, and reverted her to the normal evasiveness of the aborigines, whose greatest weapon, as with all, is laughter. To further questions, Meena answered with giggles which were not the genuine reflection of her mood, and presently Wootton dismissed her.

'Can't make her out,' he complained to Bony. 'Good looking

wench like that. Any white man could have done worse than marry her. I'd marry her myself if I'd half the chance.'

'You are not married?'

'Was. Been a widower for fourteen years. Joking, of course. Those Indian Summers I read about once don't work out. Besides ...'

'Go on,' urged Bony, laughing. 'An Indian Summer could be an improvement on Hoary Winter.'

'Not for me. I know what the heat's like. I lived in hell for twenty-two years. I know all about temperatures. Well, I'd better go along and give the men their orders. I'll tell Bill to wait about for you.'

Wootton left by one of the two pairs of french windows, and Bony dallied on at table, sipping coffee and smoking.

He wasn't happy about Wootton. He was an odd man out in this setting of Lake Eyre. He was like a newly cut diamond in an old-fashioned gold ring, and what was that saying about new wine in old bottles ... exploding? Five years he had been in this country, and he wasn't assimilated by it as fully as some immigrants in much less time. It could be a streak of pomposity. He would dig into the background.

There was the question of Mrs Bell's body. Rising, he crossed to the chair under the wall telephone and called for Constable Pierce.

'You, Inspector!' Pierce said from Loaders Springs. 'Yes, sir, what can I do? Run out there to report?'

'Perhaps. I have the copies of your reports and the statements, and I am edging myself into the picture. I am speaking softly in order not to be overheard. You hear me all right?'

'Quite clear, sir.'

'You have still in your possession the plaster casts you took of Yorky's tracks?'

'Yes, a copy. The originals, and the bullet from the body, I sent down to Adelaide.'

'When first you saw the body it was in the woman's room?'

'Yes, on the bed.'

'Did you touch the body? Then or subsequently?'

'No. Dr Crouch was with me.'

57

'Could you fetch Dr Crouch to your phone?'

'Expect so. Shall I send for him?'

'Yes, do. I'll hold the line. See that I'm not cut off.'

Bony was waiting when Meena came in with her clearing tray, and Bony waved her out. He left the instrument for the few seconds necessary to cross to the door and close it, and smiled at the picture of Meena's face. He hadn't long to wait before a deep voice spoke.

'Dr Crouch speaking, Inspector.'

'Ah! Good morning, doctor! I won't keep you long. Recall to mind, please, what happened on your arrival here. You found the body of Mrs Bell in her room. Who was with you?'

'Pierce and Wootton.'

'Finding the woman obviously dead, you turned the body over to examine the wound, I presume. Who was then with you in the room?'

'I told Pierce the woman was dead. Wootton looked ill. I asked Pierce to take Wootton away. He did so. No one was with me when I examined the body. You make me curious.'

'I'll satisfy your curiosity one day, doctor. Meanwhile, be patient with me. You found the body lying on its back under a sheet?'

'Yes.'

'How did you leave the body at the termination of the examination? I mean position.'

'On its back ... under the sheet as I found it.'

'Later that day it was removed to your station wagon. Who conveyed the body to the car?'

'I don't know, Inspector. I gave orders for it to be transferred from the house to the car.'

'Tell me this. To examine the bullet wound in the woman's back you had to cut away the clothing?'

'Yes.'

'Tell me just what you did do.'

A little impatiently, Crouch described how he had with scissors cut the white linen blouse from the back of the neck to the band of the skirt. The wound was such that it wasn't necessary at that time to examine the body further for secondary wounds, as the wound between the shoulders was obviously fatal. And Dr Crouch was now even more curious. Suavely, Bony asked him to stand by to permit Pierce access to the telephone. To Pierce he said:

'When you first saw the body, Wootton was with you. What exactly did you do? Don't tell me what the doctor did. I know.'

'Well, I entered the room, having been informed by Bray that Mrs Bell's body was there. The doctor was with me, and so was Mr Wootton. I turned down the sheet to establish the fact that the body was actually there on the bed. Mr Wootton gave a sort of moan, and Dr Crouch told me to take him out. Which I did.'

'The body was lying . . . in what position?'

'On its back, Inspector.'

'No other person entered the room while the doctor was there?'

'No; Wootton sat on a chair in the hall, and I was with him.'

'Now we come to the removal of the body to the doctor's car. Who supervised that task?'

'I did. I had Arnold Bray and Eric Maundy with me.'

'What did you do?'

'Well the body was under the sheet again,' Pierce said with slight stoicism. 'I tucked the top sheet about the body, and turned up the edges of the under sheet about the body, and the men carried it out.'

'No one of you three men saw the body?'

'No. It was as I said. No one looks at a body unless he has to.'

'That'll be all for the moment, Pierce. Come out today. Better make it for lunch. I'll tell Wootton you'll be here.'

'I'll be there, sir.'

'Good! And bring those plaster casts.'

Bony left by the window, and, crossing the square, found William Harte on the narrow veranda of the quarters. Harte was attaching a new silk cracker to his stock-whip, and his bright eyes gleamed with shrewd expectancy at Bony's approach. Having seen Arnold in the open motor shed, and the other two stockmen riding from the yards, Bony knew that he had Harte to himself, and, nodding the day's greeting, he leaned against the veranda rail, and fell to rolling the inevitable cigarette.

'How long have you been in this Lake Eyre country?' was his opening.

'All me life. Was born away over on Clifton Hills.'

'You must know it well,' conceded Bony. 'Is there any shadow of doubt in your mind that those tracks behind the meat-house were made by Yorky?'

The bright eyes became mere dark spots in the leather face.

'If them tracks were imitations, then they were ruddy good, Inspector. You're raisin' the doubts, not me. I don't think . . .'

'Supposing I told you that those tracks hadn't been left by Yorky, would you gamble your way?'

Harte took time before replying :

'No, I don't think I would, Inspector. Not now.'

'Even though Wootton saw Yorky at the blacks' camp that morning? Knew he was to head this way?'

The slow grin twitching the corners of the man's mouth supported the shrewdness Bony had already attributed to him.

'I'd say Yorky made 'em, but I wouldn't do no betting on it. There wasn't enough of those particular tracks to make me bet my shirt they was made by Yorky.'

'We'll leave it, Bill. Another matter. You saw Mrs Bell's body lying on the ground near the house. Can you recall the size and shape of the bloodstain on her blouse?'

'Too right. I won't forget that ever. The crows had made a mess of her neck and shoulders, but the blouse wasn't torn.'

Dark brown eyes and deep blue eyes held steady for a long moment.

'Between ourselves,' Bony asked, slowly.

'It's your hand,' agreed Harte.

'Draw me a picture of that bloodstain.'

Harte crouched to the earth floor of the veranda and with the point of his clasp knife granted the request.

NINE

TO RUN IS TO CRAWL

CONSTABLE PIERCE came, lunched with Wootton and Bony, teased Meena and complimented Sarah, and after two hours in conference with Bony, departed for Loaders Springs. The journey homeward seemed to him of short duration, so much was his mind occupied by impressions which confounded all preconceptions of the man he had met.

Bony was waiting in the shade of the ridge pine trees for the men to come in from the duties assigned to them that morning. He could see them, stringing down the background slopes, riding tired and thirsty horses, and he watched them free their mounts to drink or take a sand-bath. In addition to the four white men there were now four aborigines. There was no fraternizing, the aborigines taking buckets to the reservoir tanks and washing in readiness for dinner.

Pierce had left food for thought as well as the plaster casts duplicating those he had sent down to Adelaide. Bony had gathered much to add to the policeman's tersely written reports, especially material assisting him to fill in mere sketches of people and places.

Now Ole Fren Yorky stood clear to Bony, who had never seen him. Pierce had revealed the man in a light less shadowed than he had been in a report of a murder suspect, for the policeman living in a small community is able to be far less isolated than when he lives in a large community. The few are neighbours; the many animated units.

Pierce had been stationed at Loaders Springs for eleven years. He was able to say that Yorky was well behaved when in town, and this opinion was not affected by Yorky's weaknesses, one being that although he had a room at the hotel, he could be found sleeping on the bench outside, and on two occasions in winter had been discovered sleeping in a station cell.

Bony was informed of matters he would not without necessity enter into a report. He said that the previous owners of Mount Eden were confident that Meena, Sarah's daughter, was begotten by Yorky. He said, too, that long before he came to Loaders Springs, Yorky had been a participant in several brawls, and he drew the picture of a man who, although of small physique, had been dynamite in his prime. People are so apt to see a man as he is, and forget what he was.

It is obvious that a man in Pierce's situation would have opinions and theories which he could not reveal to a superior unless asked to do so. And Bony had seldom found co-operation withheld by such as Constable Pierce, who found pleasure in giving it.

'There's men who tease Yorky about his height,' Pierce had said. 'Tales told about him like this one. Yorky carried a swag bigger than himself, and once when he was walking to Loaders with a swag up, he passed right through the place because he couldn't see it for the swag! There's another story of him being in a crowded bar all evening, and towards closing time a feller said to him: 'Hullo, Yorky! Haven't seen you in years!' and Yorky said he'd been standing before him for the last two hours.

'So what have we? A wisp of a man who once could fight his way out from under a heap of he-men, and had become old and conscious of his loss of physical strength. A little man always resentful of chipping about his size. Of late years he had to bottle up what at one time had been released with fists and boots. Gradually he turned more to the aborigines and farther from the whites. He could have resented something Wootton said quite innocently, or something said by the men, even something said or not done by Mrs Bell. They're all agin' him. So he decided to steal something loved by everyone . . . young Linda. And when Mrs Bell stepped into it, he killed her.'

'Tell me about the men. Anything against them?' Bony had asked, and Pierce had replied:

'Nothing much. Young Lawton's been in trouble once or twice. Fights over the young lubras, chiefly. The last time

Canute complained about him, I told Lawton that if it happened again I would advise Canute to sool all his bucks on to him and compel him to leave the district. Once I had to serve a summons on Bray for not complying with the Taxation Regulation, and Bill Harte took to a couple of roughs passing through town who held him up for money.' Pierce chuckled. 'You should have seen them. Crouch had to nurse 'em for a couple of days before he could turn them loose.'

'Ah! Dr Crouch!'

'Yair. A character. Three-bottles-of-whisky-per-day man. Bets on flies crawling up a window. Tall, powerful man with a grouch agin' the Government, no matter what government. And is such a doctor that, did I arrest him, the entire district would set out to tar and feather me.'

'And Wootton, Pierce?'

'Told me he'd been a general storekeeper in New South. Came to Australia forty-odd years ago. Made good. Married and had two sons. Both of them joined the Army, and both were killed in action. That killed the wife. Wootton wanted to be a pastoralist, always wanted to be the big landowner, so he sold his business and bought Mount Eden.'

'And Mrs Bell?'

'Nice little woman. Wootton engaged her through an agency in Adelaide. We found out that her husband had left her a couple of years before. My wife liked her. But then my wife likes everyone. She lets out my prisoners sometimes if they spin a good tale, and I've got to go after 'em and bring them in again.'

So, over to Bony. The Law had had no troubles worth telling with Canute and his people. Canute and several of the Elders, including Murtee, wore clothes but were almost as distant from white influence as are the wild abos. The younger people like Meena and Charlie and Rex, were civilized and reasonably well educated, thanks to the Missioner, but nevertheless were rigidly controlled by their Elders.

Although it was now late and Sarah would ring the dinner gong any minute, the afternoon continued hot and still. The crows were waking into activity, and Bony idly watched three of them coming from across the lake while he continued to ponder on the character sketches presented by Constable Pierce. A willi-willi, red and dense and powerful, its column of dust and debris revolving at terrific speed, marched down the western dunes to the lake. Lake Eyre refused to feed it. It first cut off the willi's feet, then its legs, then masticated the swaying body, working upwards until only the head was left wagging stupidly a thousand yards high.

Here, in this land, to run was to crawl. In this land, the ancient legends were reality; the lake was dead, but the surrounding land was sleeping under the hot sun, waiting for the water to return and transform its dust into verdancy.

Another night came to comfort men as a cloak for the naked, and when another day dawned, Bony was astride his horse and travelling northward from Mount Eden.

He followed the cement-hard white beach, flanked on one side by embankments of red sand, and on the other by the sea of rusty mud. Here and there the tracks of cattle told where animals had ventured on to the mud a few yards to lick the salt from its crust. He came at long intervals to the mouth of an ancient river, or to the lip of an inlet. The land constantly changed for him; the sea of mud never. The only thing lacking in this picture was water. Given water to hide the mud, to cool the breeze, this beach could be named Crescent Parade, and this one ahead Little Cove, and the one traversed a natural for a Nudist Colony.

When Yorky with the child had left Mount Eden, he would have kept to this iron-hard shore, knowing that even the aborigines could not track them, and knowing, too, that he would have to step from it at some place or other, and that the aborigines would know that as well. He had certainly won a remarkable victory. He would have been guided by the Universal Controller of Life, Water.

Bony found no sand-soakage in the creek beds. Once he walked out on the mud, when his feet sank ankle-deep into it, and with a digging stick he holed down to the clay bed, and found no seepage.

Towards sundown he saw ahead a line of dots extending on

to the lake. The dots grew to black columns, collapsed to become a row of drunken aborigines, and finally became fence posts, extending for a mile out, and the fence must have been hastily erected years back, following the swift slaughter of this inland sea. However, near the 'coast' new wires had been strung to keep Mount Eden cattle within the boundary, for this was the boundary fence once patrolled by Ole Fren Yorky, and which Bony now determined to follow, to examine Yorky's camps.

This night he spent beside a small iron hut near a bore. There was a gate here giving egress to the unfenced country to the north. Inside the hut were several thirty-gallon oil tanks now containing weevilly flour, and small tins of tea and sugar, matches and plug tobacco, light rope, tar in bottles, and kerosene in a tin; without doubt a camelman's camp.

The following night Bony spent at another of Yorky's camps, this time a three-sided shed constructed with tree branches, and situated on the bank of a creek where water lay a foot deep above coarse sand. Long after the water had disappeared it could be obtained by digging.

At neither of these two camps was there sign of human visitors. Bony had seen no human tracks beside the netted fence. He had observed no smoke signals, no suspicious movements amid the prevailing mirage, which hemmed him all day long.

Next morning, the first warning stirred the hairs at the back of his neck. During the afternoon he was convinced that he was being followed. And when he camped again at one of Yorky's old camps he was elated by his first evidence since he began this investigation, of the sand dune coming to him.

It was the third night from the homestead, and he slept in a single blanket on a claypan some hundred yards from the glowing embers of the camp fire. He was undisturbed, and started the following day before sun-up, keeping to the fence, his destination the next watering place but a mile from the road to Loaders Springs, the fence having followed a great arc.

At noon he was still being trailed, and knew that the tracker was keeping several miles behind him. It was unnecessary for the tracker to see what he did, where he went, for the tracks left by his horses, and his own when he dismounted, would be easily read.

In a city, of course, you slip around a corner and wait to see who comes after you. But how to deal with an Australian sleuth who maintains his distance from you by many miles?

On coming to a mile-wide flat bearing nothing but foothigh tussock grass, Bony decided to wait for the tracker beyond the low sand ridges on the far side.

As anticipated, the terrain was suitable. He tethered his horses on a patch of wild rye amid a small area of wait-a-bit and box trees, and himself lay at ease in the shade cast by a cotton bush. Before him was the flat, gently pulsating in the ground mirage. He could see the opposing ridges over which he had crossed to ride down to the flat.

An eagle came low to prospect him and the horses. He waved a hand to tell the bird there was nothing dead, and the eagle soared aloft to continue its eternal aerial patrol. Bony was lucky that the crows hadn't followed him from the last camp, and that no others had yet taken up their espionage.

It is ever an advantage to know what the enemy knows and does not know. The tracker knew that Bony was travelling from one of Yorky's water camps to the next. Therefore, he could not know that Bony was now waiting for him. On the other hand, he would not know if Bony decided to deviate, chose to make temporary camp to brew tea, or take a nap, and so he would proceed with extreme caution, and when coming to the first flat he would watch for signs that his quarry could be lingering just beyond it.

As usual at this time, the day was hot, and humidity low, the shade temperature at the distant homestead being in the vicinity of 120 degrees. There was no wind, and against the golden-dusted sky individual clouds were born, grew to giants, dwindled to dwarfs and died. They first appeared as white dots, swiftly extending, thus creating great shadows laden with cool air, and bringing about the disturbances fashioning the strictly local windstorms called willi-willies.

The favoured march of the willi-willies is from north to

south, and they were travelling this line, not many being in sight at the same time, seldom more than three. One passed close to Bony, whipping his hair and drying the perspiration on his face. It moved with steady speed at about thirty miles an hour, whirling sand and debris upward into its red body, roaring like a beast when passing over the scrub. Yet another halted on the flat, performed a jig, rocked as if about to collapse with fatigue, finally became thrice in size and reached high speed as though a living thing.

What with the heat, the sticky flies, the eagles and the willi-willies, Bony was left with no cause for boredom. With the patience of his maternal ancestors, he waited, and was beginning to believe he would still be waiting the next day when a feminine willi-willi came tripping to the distant sand ridges. She paused there, seemingly shrinking from the open space, a little fearful of venturing farther. Then, mustering courage, she advanced cautiously.

Wisps of dead grass and herbage formed her feet, shimmered her red gown with gold to the waist. Her slim body rose to several hundred feet, swaying gently in a swooning waltz as she proceeded. A gambler here would be in paradise, for he could back his hunch without taking into account pulled horses or stacked cards, and Bony was backing this willi-willi to pass on his left, when the unpredictable happened.

As they are conceived by a gentle eddy so the willies die in an eddy. This one began to die when but a hundred yards from Bony. Something gross and unsporting punched her in the tummy, but she staggered onward in increasing tempo as though striving to keep up with the orchestra.

Bony betted she wouldn't reach his side of the flat, and won. Suddenly she lost her head, and lifted her skirt as though to cover her shamed head.

Absorbed in the fate of the female, he saw not the male, for there was Charlie racing to cover, he having almost crossed the flat in the centre of a revolving column of sand.

TEN

IN EFFORT TO TRADE

BETRAYED BY the willi-willi, Charlie gained the nearest cover at Olympic speed, ending the spring with a dive for Bony's cotton bush.

Following the dieting of the walkabout to the Neales River, Charlie had fattened on Sarah's white-man tucker, and was now in excellent condition, his arms and legs of Grecian proportions, his tummy less to be admired. All he wore was a pair of dark-brown shorts; his only equipment a hessian bag subsequently found to contain a small calico bag of tea and a gnawed leg of fire-charred kangaroo. On coming to rest under the cotton bush, his head was within fifteen inches of Bony's head. When their gaze clashed, Bony said mildly:

'Good day-ee, Charlie! Are you travelling?'

Charlie grinned, genuine humour associated with astonishment in his black eyes.

'Day-ee, Mr Bonaparte. Bit hot in the sun, eh?' Then realization of the situation smote him and he shrank away without thought of the sunlight burning his feet beyond the bush. 'Crikey! This your bush, eh? I'll get going.'

'We go together,' purred Bony, standing with Charlie. 'We have much to talk about, and three miles' travel to the next camp. We go that way, to my horses.'

Charlie found dislike of the hard blue eyes and of the automatic directed to his stomach, and ultimately disliked the hard smile on Bony's face. He was ordered to unhitch the packhorse and lead it to Yorky's next camp, and on glancing backward now and then, it was to see Bony mounted, the pistol in his right hand. Escorted occasionally by an indifferent williwilli, they moved over the flats and the low sand ridges, through the swamp gums, across dry creek beds and narrower gutters, to arrive at a bough shed erected beside a lake of shallow water maintained by a bore half a mile away.

Here Bony told Charlie to remove the load from the pack-horse. Then with his left hand he unstrapped one of the pack-bags and took from it a pair of handcuffs. They were not of the kind Charlie had seen previously, which are manacles rather than wrist-cuffs. Still, he knew their purpose, and he offered no resistance. The heavy pack-saddle was lifted into the shade of the bough shed, and then, before he understood what was going on, one of the cuffs was unlocked from a wrist and relocked to the iron structure of the pack saddle. Thus he had one hand free with which to protect his face from the flies, and if he wanted to run, well, the saddle went with him, and he wouldn't run far and never fast.

Save for its proximity to water, the camp site was unsatisfactory, open to the westerlies, unprotected from the dusty ground churned by the hoofs of nomadic cattle. Although brackish, the water was good enough for tea if taken with plenty of sugar, and the closer to the bore, so was the water more heavily laden with alkali, hot almost to boiling point at the mouth of the L-shape iron outlet pipe. Day and night gushed the water from the depths, year after year since the bore was put down.

Bony made tea, gave Charlie a pannikin of it, opened a tin of beef for each of them. He tossed the charred kangaroo leg to the already gathered crows, and then when they were smoking and the sun had gone down, he began the interrogation.

'You're a rotten tracker, Charlie. Too much Mission learning, eh? You learn to read and write, but you're no tracker.'

'I followed you all the way from Mount Eden, anyway,' reminded Charlie, cheerfully, and yet with wariness in his eyes. 'I done no wrong. Free country. Mr Wootton go crook when he knows about this.' He raised his cuffed wrist, and for the first time anger glowed. 'I got my School Certificate, like Meena and the others. I'll write to the Chief Protector of Aborigines in Adelaide.'

'Do that, Charlie,' Bony said kindly. 'Ask him to call on you in jail. You see, Charlie, I'm a terrible liar. I'm the worst liar you ever met. I may – it will depend on you – arrest you and

69

put you up on a charge of interfering with a police officer in the execution of his duty, obstructing the police, assaulting a police officer, taking unlawful refuge inside a willi-willi, and several other matters I could think of.'

'You got to prove all that.'

Charlie was as yet unimpressed, because his respect for Constable Pierce was due to that policeman's tolerance, and also to the result of a little learning and association with a Missioner. Evil white men hadn't entered his ken. On the opposite side, Bony knew all too well that you cannot abstract with violence information from an unwilling aborigine. He was sure that Charlie hadn't tracked him of his own volition, that he had been ordered to do so, and most likely was instructed not to divulge who issued the order.

'You know Constable Pierce, Charlie,' Bony went on. 'Some other place boss policeman over Constable Pierce, and some other place bigger boss policeman. Now I am a Big Chief policeman. I'm like Chief Canute. What I say goes. I tell lies about you and everyone believes me, not you. You tell the judge I'm a big-feller liar, and he'll add six months more jail. I say you did all these things, and you go to jail for three years. Better for you to tell me where Yorky is, and then instead of jail Constable Pierce will make you his tracker.'

'Sez you,' scoffed Charlie, and Bony was dismayed because Charlie now appeared to be more sophisticated than he had thought.

'You must have been to the pictures,' he said.

'Too right! Down at Loaders Springs. Us Mission abos was allowed by the Missioner every Sat'day night. Took us to town in his truck. We seen Bob Mitchum and Gary Cooper and all them.'

'You astonish me, Charlie. The cinema on Saturday night and hiding in a willi-willi on Sunday morning. Singing in church on Sunday evening, and pointing the bone on Monday afternoon. Still, you'll be seeing films in jail once every month, and singing songs when locked in a nice cold cell at night. And, Charlie, while you're in jail, do you know what will happen?'

'What?'

'Some other aborigine is going to take Meena.'

With boosted confidence, Charlie countered with:

'Meena belongs to Canute. No blackfeller can take Meena.'

'But you tried, Charlie. I saw you the other night. She slapped your face, and then let you kiss her. She let you kiss her twice when you made the doll of her and gave it to Linda. I know you like Meena. I know that she likes you, too. But you're afraid, aren't you? You're afraid of old Canute. You know that if you run away with Meena, the bucks will track you and catch you, and you will be speared, and Meena's knees will be broken so that she can't run away another time.'

The scenting nostrils were flaring, for love and desire are not the prerogatives of the white man. Almost dreamily, Bony went on talking.

'You want to marry Meena, Charlie, and old Canute say: "No, you don't. Meena's my woman. I got her when she was a baby. I bought her from her father." D'you know who Meena's father was?'

Charlie frowned, then shook his head.

'Does Sarah know?'

Now Charlie grinned, saying:

'She'd know nothing like that for sure.'

'Then who did Canute get Meena from when she was born? I don't think Meena was promised to Canute ever. I think it's a yarn. Having visited the white man's halls of culture called "the pictures", you'll have heard the word "Sucker" and will know just what it means. You, Charlie, Sucker Charlie.

'Long time ago, and when I look back I'm astonished how far back on my tracks it was, I met my Meena,' continued Bony, and instantly Charlie's interest was increased. 'My Meena was lovely and soft and warm, just like your Meena could be for you. But my Meena made out she didn't want me. You know, let me kiss her on the tip of her nose and only that. You know what these Meenas are, I'm sure.

'Well, a long time went by, and I only ever got as far as kissing my Meena on the tip of her nose. Then one day the Missioner came, and I asked him straight if he'd marry me to my Meena. When he said "Yes," I grabbed my Meena and ran her to the Missioner, and he read out the words, and when he asked me if I would, I said, "Yes," and when he asked my Meena if she would, and she wouldn't answer, I pinched her bottom till she did. D'you know what I did then?'

Celibate Charlie was caught.

'I dragged my Meena away from the Mission, and away from the camp, and soon she didn't have to be dragged any more. She ran with me, and presently we came to a creek. Beside the creek was a great place where tobacco bush grew all round a billabong, and among the bush were ducks laying eggs, and waterhens mating, and ibis standing in the water catching silver bream. Then I made a humpy of bush and gathered leaves to make the ground soft and warm. And d'you know what, Charlie?'

'What?' pressed the entranced Charlie.

'Why, now I've got one son who's a doctor missioner away up in Queensland, and two more sons as well. Of course, you won't have any sons, and you won't have any Meena in a nice warm humpy. Because you'll be in jail. That's if you won't tell me what I want to know. Then what? Why, Meena will be looking for Charlie, and Charlie will be locked up in jail, and then she'll come to thinking she'd like to have babies, and some other blackfeller will be waiting for her, and he won't be so silly as to make me lock him up in jail.'

By no means without imagination Charlie pictured his Meena in the arms of a rival while he himself languished in durance vile. He had never been in a whitefeller's jail, but he knew there were no women in them, and once there he couldn't go on walkabout whenever inherited instincts commanded.

Seated on the ground, he rested his back against the pack-saddle, and by bringing his free hand close to the cuffed one, he managed to roll a cigarette and strike a match. It was almost dark, but the air was still heated by the hot earth. The stars were dancing their summer jig. A wedge of ducks whirred low, decided that the artificial lake was too small, and sped upward and away into the profound silence. Now and then Bony fed the small fire from Yorky's reserve woodpile, and the reflection of the lazy flames shimmered upon both faces, framing them within the shape of the bough shed.

Wise in the ways of the bush and its inhabitants, yet Bony was tricked. He had thought it possible that Charlie would be tracking him in company with a mate, but as the hours passed, and as Charlie had evinced no confidence in rescue, Bony dismissed the thought. His mind being intent on manoeuvring Charlie into a mood of co-operation at least, and full confession at most, he was unaware of the stalker.

And as it turned out, so was Charlie.

Bony's task was not an easy one. He could meet a white man and know exactly how to deal with him. He could have met a wild black man and would have known how to deal with him too. In either case, a matter of plain psychology based on the race and character of the subject. Although Charlie was a pure-blooded aborigine, he was a complex being, occupying a place between the wild aborigine and his inhibitions and superstitions, and the fully civilized aborigines who in many districts near the cities of Australia are justly entitled to 'Mister' and 'Missus'.

Therefore: how much was Charlie influenced by Canute and the Elders supporting the chief, and how much by the Missioner and Mr Wootton and Constable Pierce? Bony believed that by placing Charlie midway between these two groups, then moving him half way to the left towards Canute and his Elders, he would have Charlie correctly positioned.

'I tell you something, Charlie,' he said, when Charlie gave no sign of co-operation. 'Suppose you say you are my friend. Then I can't tell old Canute how you made a mess of tracking me, and I won't say anything about that to anyone else. Then all the lubras and the little gins won't laugh like hell at you. So we say nothing about that, and you tell me why you been tracking me, eh?'

Charlie mutely shook his head, with a faint sign of reluctance, and Bony added to the bribe.

'Suppose I tackle old Canute, Charlie. Suppose I tell him I know he and Murtee been pointing the bone, and that I'll have them put into jail for it. Who did they point the bone at last time?'

'Dunno,' replied Charlie. 'Perhaps it was at old Moses over on Titigi. Perhaps it was up on the Neales. Anyhow, old Moses he died pretty quick.'

'That's it,' agreed Bony. 'Well, I tell Canute he and Murtee pointed the bone at Moses. Old Moses died. That's murder, Charlie. So I tell Canute like this. I say: "Look you, Canute, old feller, you're too old to take Meena and Charlie loves Meena, and Meena loves Charlie, and they want to be married by the Missioner, all straight and square." Then old Canute he say: "You go to hell. I got Meena when she was born. Meena's my woman." And I say: "All right, Canute, then you go off to jail for all your life. I know you murdered old Moses by pointing the bone at him, and I'll tell the white feller judge all about it. Then you'll be hung.

' "Now I'll tell you what, you silly old coot. You let Charlie have Meena, him being a young feller and able to look after her, and I'll say nothing about you pointing the bone at Moses." ' Bony smiled at Charlie, and Charlie was seeing a little of the light of common sense. 'Do we trade?'

'No,' countered someone behind Bony. 'You take that thing off Charlie's wrist. Go on, take it off.'

Swiftly Bony turned. He found himself looking into the barrel of his own automatic. The barrel was wavering, and the safety catch was still on. Above the hand holding the pistol was the face of Canute's Meena.

ELEVEN

BONY'S GUESTS

ACCORDING TO persons who are brought to trial for murder, guns go off of themselves, and quite often a jury actually believes it. Anyone who has the slightest acquaintance with firearms knows that you must pull the trigger to discharge such a weapon, and to do that you have to curl a finger about the trigger. Still fewer people appear to understand that many types of firearms are fitted with a safety device, and that if the safety catch is in position no amount of trigger-pulling will bring about the desired explosion.

When Meena pointed the automatic pistol at Bony, it was instantly obvious that either she was ignorant of this type of weapon or had no intention of permitting it to go off of itself and commit murder. Her wide eyes and stern mouth, although presenting a new facet of her dark beauty, warned Bony that he was fortunate that the weapon she held was not a waddy, for waddies are also claimed to rise and fall of themselves, but are much less lethal.

'Why, Meena!' he exclaimed. 'What a pleasant surprise.'

'You loose that Charlie,' she commanded. 'Go on! I'll count three and then . . .' threatened Meena.

Lazily Bony turned to one side and took the cuff key from his side pocket. Tossing it to Meena's feet he said:

'You loose him. I'm tired.'

Her left hand went down for the key, and from a crouching position she knelt, and on her knees made the short journey to Charlie. Arrived at the saddle and his imprisoned wrist, she put the pistol on the ground, and the next instant it was whisked away by Bony. Meena was up on her feet enraged and shouting, and the pistol was pointing at her. Her shouting faded to a whimper of fury, when Bony said:

'You must never place a delicate weapon like a pistol on the dusty ground. Look at all the dust and sand on it. I'll have to spend half an hour cleaning it. Now you free Charlie, then put more wood on the fire and boil the billy for tea. And don't let the sand get into those handcuffs. Put them into the pack-bag, and give me the key before you lose it. Women!' Charlie stood perplexed, as was Meena, and Bony went on:

'Sit down again, Charlie, and roll a cigarette. We have a cook now, remember. She makes the tea.'

From staring at each other, they stared at Bony, who was squinting down the barrel of the pistol as though the weapon was his most precious possession. Then Charlie grunted and the tableau ended by the man sitting down and the girl looking about for the billycan.

'What d'you think of my plan to tackle old Canute?' nonchalantly inquired Bony. 'Ought to make him come to heel and give you Meena. In fact, I'll guarantee that it does. Or else, Charlie. Or else he goes to jail.'

Charlie grunted again, and looked at Meena. She had placed the filled billycan against the red fire coals and was standing and gazing at the flames in obvious amazement. Unconsciously she was now Bony's firm ally in the scheme to soften Charlie. She wore only a pair of shorts, dark blue in colour and an admirable fit. Silhouetted against the firelight, her figure was tantalizing, her naked breasts, her slim neck, her profile and the crown of curly hair all totalling the love call to Man. It stirred even Bony.

Charlie, although young, possessed wisdom. Negatively he shook his head and winked, thus advising 'no see' tactics. The girl continued to watch the flames, and Bony began to hum a tune and apply himself industriously to the pistol-cleaning. The water in the billy boiled, and the girl dropped a handful of leaves into it, then lifting the billy with a short stick under its handle, she set it down to cool, and turned to look at the two men.

'Charlie, stir yourself and open a tin of meat for Meena,' ordered Bony. 'Come and sit down, Meena, and let Charlie look after you. You must be hungry and thirsty.'

Charlie scrambled off to obey, and Meena sank to the soft earth, sat tailor-wise, and looked at Bony as though he were the man that never was. Carefully, Bony wrapped the pistol in the rag.

'I should not have left this on the blanket roll behind me. It might have gone off when you picked it up, Meena. I don't like pistols. Dangerous things to handle. How did you know that Charlie and I were camped here?'

'Tracked you easy enough,' boasted Meena. 'Saw where you caught Charlie just off the flat and made him lead the pack-horse.' She accepted the opened tin of meat from Charlie without looking at him, and when he brought her a pannikin of tea, still she ignored him. 'You're a cunning feller, Mr Bonaparte. You catch Charlie like he was a little gin.'

'He had bad luck, Meena. You see, he was crossing that flat inside a willi-willi, and just before the willi got to my side it fell apart, and there he was in the open. Very nearly tricked me. I've heard of it being done, but not seen it before, and I've never tried it. What's it like, Charlie, inside?'

'All right,' chuckled Charlie. 'Air's clear. Sand rushing round and round that fast you can just see out. Meena's done it. I watched her. That time she went along good till the willi went faster and faster, and she run and run to keep with it, and then she fell down, and there she was.'

'And here she is,' added Bony. 'Who were you tracking, Meena? Charlie or me?'

'Charlie? What for you track Mr Bonaparte? Go on, you tell. I saw you start after him at the homestead, and I said to Sarah I'd find out for why.'

Charlie was now an ebony image. The firelight on the girl's face and body was reflected as from gold dust. That she was famished for food and drink was plain, and Bony sought information.

'You have been on Charlie's tracks for three days, Meena?'

She nodded, and continued to glare at Charlie.

'And no tucker?'

Still glaring at Charlie, impatiently she shook her head. To her lover she said:

77

'You're a cunning feller, too, but not properly cunning. I heard what Mister Bonaparte said he'd do to Canute about me, and I seen you go all softy-softy thinking about it. You're going to say what Mister Bonaparte wants, and you're not going to get me off of Canute for doing it, see?'

Charlie looked embarrassed, and began pouring sand from one hand to the other. He employed the old, old stratagem of laughing to cover up, and Meena threw the meat tin with deadly aim, the tin smashing into Charlie's mouth.

'But Charlie is happy, Meena. He and I were having a little talk before you butted in.'

Blood showed on the man's lips where the jagged edge of the tin had connected. He licked off the blood and stood, for now primitive man was set upon his dignity, and primitive woman was to pay forfeit. Perhaps.

'Before you begin, put more wood on the fire,' Bony requested calmly.

'I'll do that,' roared Charlie, and Meena yelled: 'And I will, too.'

'All right, but don't put all of Yorky's woodpile on,' Bony shouted.

They calmed, both panting less from exertion than from consuming anger, and they regarded Bony, who still reclined at ease on the warm earth. The look in his eyes probably reminded them of the Missioner, and something of the Missioner's teaching, for with downcast eyes Meena dropped her load of wood and returned to sit close to Bony, to torment Charlie, rather than for protection, of which she wished none. The lover flung his wood on the flames, which quickly grew, and sullenly he sat down with his back to the saddle.

'Now we are together again,' murmured Bony, 'let us be at peace and talk friendly. True, Meena, that you tracked Charlie to find out why he tracked me?'

'That's right.' From the pocket of her shorts she took a tin, from which she produced tobacco and papers and began making a cigarette. He waited, and then leaned forward to offer the flame. She leaned nearer to bring the cigarette to the match, and smiled provocatively at Charlie.

78

'And why have you been tracking me?' Bony hurriedly demanded of Charlie.

Charlie took refuge in sullenness, and Meena said brightly:

'That ole Canute feller sent him, I bet.'

'Like to know, wouldn't you?' Charlie asked with a feeble imitation of a sneer, and Bony now decided to break up this lovers' tiff.

'Now listen, you two. Playing about tracking each other and running around inside willi-willies is over for today. There's Yorky and Linda Bell. There's the policeman and Mr Wootton and me. You are supposed to be as anxious as anyone to locate Yorky. Now, Charlie, you answer questions and no more silliness. What we all say to one another goes no farther than the firelight, I promise you. And don't forget, you two have been playing each other too long. You have to get married by the Missioner, settle down, have children, be happy. I'll fix Canute, don't worry. All right, Charlie, why have you been tracking me?'

'Murtee tell me I track you, I see where you go and what you do,' replied Charlie, still sullen.

'But you were working for the station.'

'I told Boss I was sick.'

'What did Mr Wootton say?'

'Nothing. But he put Bill Harte on to tracking me, see if I was sick.' Charlie laughed. 'Soon lost Bill Harte.'

'How do you know Mr Wootton put Bill Harte on to you?'

'I seen Bill ridin' slow-like behind me. He was keeping to cover.'

'And Mr Wootton told Bill Harte to track you? How do you know that?'

'He musta. Bill never heard me tell Boss I was sick.'

'All right, leave that. Murtee told you to track me along. Why did he tell you to do that?'

'Dunno. Murtee Medicine Man.'

'Has Murtee got Linda's dolls?'

The question certainly surprised Charlie, and Meena said:

'Course not. Linda's dolls are in her playhouse.'

'Two of them are. Ole Fren Yorky and Meena are not.

79

They're gone. Someone took them. Who?'

'No blackfeller took 'em,' asserted Charlie, and Meena watched him like a suspicious wife. She said:

'I'll tell Sarah. Sarah'll find out. Maybe Mr Wootton, or one of the men took them. Them dolls belonged to Linda.'

'Too right,' agreed Charlie. 'I made 'em.'

'Where are Yorky and Linda? You tell me.'

Reaction to this question satisfied Bony for the moment. He put another searcher.

'How many trucks went up to the Neales for your trackers?'

'Two. Arnold and Jim Holly from over Wandirna.'

'You all came back on those trucks?'

'All the men, and some of the lubras. Meena and Sarah and others.'

'Well, then, who stayed behind, to walk back?'

Charlie rolled off a dozen names, including Canute, and further questioning disclosed a doubt in Charlie's mind that Murtee was in the camp when the trucks came. He had not returned to the homestead on either of the trucks, both Charlie and Meena were sure. They saw Murtee two days afterwards in the camp by the creek. Canute was there, too, and they spent most of every day rubbing churinga stones against their foreheads and squatting over a little fire well apart from the others.

'When you got back, Meena, what did you do? Go tracking for Yorky, too?'

'No. Sarah was put to cooking at the homestead, me to help her and look after the house. Plenty of people about then.'

'You don't know where Yorky and Linda went?'

Meena shook her head.

'Does Sarah know?'

Again the girl replied negatively.

'Does Canute know?'

Shutters fell before her eyes. One moment they were expressive, the next moment they were blank. Charlie was frowning, and when Bony looked his way, the shutters had dropped too. Silence reigned about the fire. Above, the heavy silence was disturbed by the conversation of a wedge of ducks.

Bony pretended not to notice the fallen shutters, and went on with his questions. At once the shutters were raised and he was again receiving co-operation. He learned that Mr Wootton had not been chasing Mrs Bell. That Arnold hadn't been making up to her. That William Harte had 'put it on her' to marry him, and that Harry Lawton said he was going to push his luck. He learned, too, that Wootton had threatened to sack Harry Lawton if he went on baiting Ole Fren Yorky, imitating his voice and his peculiar manner of walking. Knowing the answer, he asked:

'Did you see Mrs Bell after she was shot?'

Both shook their heads vigorously.

'Wasn't she shot in the back?'

Both brightened at being able to answer in the affirmative.

'Made a nasty mess of her blouse, so Constable Pierce told me.'

They agreed with Constable Pierce, and nonchalantly, Bony made a mark on the ground – a question mark. On looking at them, his brows raised, they nodded.

'You never saw her,' he said. 'How d'you know?'

And the shutters fell again.

TWELVE

PRODDING THE ENEMY

ON ROUSING from an early cat-nap, the Three Sisters told Bony the time was about midnight. There were wild ducks on the bore-created pond, and he was puzzled by what could possibly interest them in water where no weeds could grow, and spent a lazy moment in reaching the conclusion that they were resting. Far away a cow bellowed, and, even farther than the cow, a pack of dingoes broke into a howling chorus.

The night was still and warm. Nearer him than the fire, Meena lay sleeping on her side, her head resting on an arm. By the pack-saddle, Charlie slept, lying on his back, his head resting on the ground. Bony dozed off again, and when he stirred next time, the Three Sisters said it was five o'clock, and dawn was tinting the east pale sea-green.

The billy was half full of the last tea brew, and this Bony heated by placing the can on the broken-open fire embers. Sipping the blue-black tea, and chain-smoking what he had the audacity to call cigarettes, he squatted over the red embers as his maternal ancestors had done, feeling about him the influences of five hundred generations of Canutes and Murtees, and their Charlies and Meenas.

He was concerned this morning by the points of conversation of the previous evening, for all the points when welded strongly indicated aboriginal participation in what appeared to be a crime in which only white people were involved.

It could be claimed that no crime committed by a white person on or against another white person in this Lake Eyre Basin could be unknown by the aborigines, for there are many who believe that nothing can happen without aboriginal knowledge, whether it be the death of an eagle or the changed shape of a sand dune. In strong support of this contention was the fact that Canute, blind as he was, saw with the eye of his mind the shape of the bloodstain on the back of the murdered woman. Canute had passed that knowledge to others of his tribe by, or with the assistance of, his dijeridoo, at the same time passing it to Bony, who had been present. Before that moment of receiving the blurred picture, which to others nearer to Canute would be clear as crystal, Bony had seen no photograph of it, nor read a description of it in any report.

It was an item of information known by Canute when he and his tribe were all supposed to be fifty miles from the scene of the crime, and as nothing can reside in a man's mind unless drawn into it from outside, from whom had he received the description of a bloodstain roughly in the form of a question mark?

When Bony had bluntly asked the man and the woman still sleeping nearby how Canute knew of that mark, shutters fell. They might now know how or from whom Canute was informed, but they did know he had been so informed, and they could have gained their knowledge in the same way and at the same time that Bony had. They would not question Canute, would accept the fact that he knew, and be content to ignore something which did not concern them.

Then why had Canute passed the knowledge to his followers? Was it to impress upon them his authority, and to confirm a ruling he and his Medicine Man had proclaimed? Where are Yorky and Linda Bell, those two sleepers had been asked, and the shutters had fallen swiftly as though he might read the answer in unguarded eyes.

This would account for lack of evidence of concern about the fate of Linda Bell. It would support the opinion that the interest of the aborigines in tracking the man and the child waned long before it could reasonably be expected to do. For your aborigine is the greatest child lover of all human races, and Bony was sure that Yorky would have been tracked right to the tip of Cape York had he murdered Linda Bell.

The rested ducks skittered across the glass-like surface of the small lake, to take off on the next leg of their journey, and within minutes it would be full light. Standing, Bony gazed on the sleeping lovers who dared not defy the authority governing their hearts and minds, and he was compelled to admire the degree of discipline to which they had been brought, and to pity them for the freedom thus denied them. He took a towel to the water, stripped and walked to the centre of the small lake, when it but reached his knees, and lowered himself into it and watched the changing lights in the sky above.

To question Charlie and his Meena further would be unfair to them, as well as futile. They had consciously and unconsciously given him something to aid his investigation. They knew a little of the much known to Canute and his Grand Vizier. They were sure in mind that Linda was safe enough. And that meant the child was still within the Lake Eyre Basin. By tracking him, Charlie was merely obeying an order. By tracking Charlie, Meena had acted on impulse prompted by one of several reasons. Neither could be rushed; both could be led to further co-operation.

Towelling himself, he dressed and returned to the camp, where he was shaving when the girl stirred and stood, stretched her arms and opened wide her shoulders. Seeing him, she turned to the fire and replenished the fuelling, then filled the billy from the pack-drum and set it against the flames.

On completing his toilet, Bony crossed to stand with her.

'After we have eaten you had better return to the homestead,' he said. 'You will remember that you didn't catch up with Charlie, and he and I will wipe out the tracks about this place to prove it.'

She turned to face him, her large dark eyes gentle, the grey flecks soft and distinct. He saw himself in her, and she herself in him. Each of the same duality of race, each was of neither one race nor the other. There was a faint tremble about her mouth when she said:

'Did you speak true last night when you told Charlie about your Meena, and being married and running away to that place among the tobacco bush?'

'Yes. You heard that?'

She nodded, her face downcast.

'You would like the Missioner to marry you and Charlie, wouldn't you?'

Again the slight nod, the dark eyes hopeful, and Bony wished that Marie, his wife, was there to help the girl to break the chains of tribal taboos.

'Canute is blind and old,' he reminded her. 'Murtee is old. I'll tell them to free you from the birth promise so that you can marry Charlie. When I tell them, they will. And then the Missioner can marry you, and you can go away and camp somewhere among tobacco bush where Charlie can love you.'

'True?'

'Bet?'

She watched him break unequally two match sticks, watched him wave his hands, then present the sticks in his clenched fist, the tops on a level.

'Long I will; short I won't,' he recited.

She pulled one of the sticks, and he opened his hand and she found her choice to be the longer. She remained so still with her head bent to look at those sticks, that he wondered if she had detected the trick which removed the gamble from the act, and then was rewarded by the smile on her face, a smile which, like the day, was slowly born.

'Better wake that Charlie,' he advised, and turned away to re-pack his shaving gear.

She wakened Charlie by nudging him with her toes and calling him a lazy black bastard. Charlie grunted, stood, stretched as she had done, grinned and lunged at her. She turned and fled, fled to the lake, and he raced after her and joined battle with splashing water. She danced about him, shouting with laughter at his attempts to grab her, shrieked with pretended terror when he succeeded. Together they fell and writhed in the foam, and eventually came walking back to camp hand in hand. And as they ate the food presented by Bony, the heat of the fire raised steam from their shorts.

Later, the two men silently watched the girl skirting the lake, and Bony thought that if white girls had been there to watch Meena, they would never wear shoes. For a moment she stood on the crest of a red dune, then turned and waved before disappearing beyond it.

'How far is the Loaders Springs road?' Bony asked, and was told some four miles. Eighteen miles beyond the road gate was the next of Yorky's camps where water lay in a rock-hole. 'You can follow on after me, Charlie. You know, make believe you're still tracking me, eh?'

Charlie laughed, and there was no doubt he was pleased at this way out of admission of failure. They discussed the matter of erasing Meena's tracks, and Charlie said it couldn't be done under two days, and predicted wind later on this day which would do the job for them. He brought the belled horses, helped to load the pack-animal, and squatted over the dying fire while giving Bony a lead of several miles.

Sitting easy in his saddle, the pack-horse trailing behind, Bony began soon to doubt that Charlie's weather prediction could be correct. The sky gave no sign of wind, and if no wind came to wipe away Meena's tracks, they would be read by another aborigine, who would report them. Noon found Bony still riding. The willi-willies were again on the march, the sun-heat powerful, and the necessity of creating a diversion from those camp tracks became even stronger.

One of Bony's rules of crime investigation, and one which more often than not brought results, was to stir up those opposed to him when it seemed they were standing still. Canute and Murtee were reclining in the tree-shade and content with the counter-move they had made by sending Charlie to find out what the big-feller policeman was doing. Charlie and the big-feller policeman were following an endless boundary fence in the heat of a late summer, a fence lying along the perimeter of a great circle centred by Mount Eden homestead. In three days Bony and his follower would again reach Lake Eyre, this time to the south of the homestead, and so far the only gain for Bony was what he had set out to achieve, proof of interest by the aborigines in his investigation.

He decided to create a diversion from Meena's tracks which also would spur those wily aborigine leaders into action of some kind.

He would smoke-signal to them!

At four o'clock the wind was still absent, and the sky was wiped clean of clouds.

The place for the signals was found in a narrow gully where grew young tobacco bush amid sapling gums. Bony heaped dry bush and sticks at three widely separated points, and beside the rubbish he deposited other heaps of green tobacco bush and green tree boughs.

In general, smoke-signalling is done to convey simple messages, and in particular is used to draw a distant medicine man or head man into telepathic communication. It was not Bony's intention to send a message, but to create confusion, curiosity and alarm.

He fired a heap of rubbish, and the rubbish burned brightly without smoke. On to this fire he tossed green bush, and at once dense smoke rose straight upward. When the column was high and the green stuff almost consumed, he fired the second heap, and when it was bright, blanketed it with green boughs. Thence from one fire to another, he sent up three columns with varied spacing of each, the weather being perfect, and he patted himself with justifiable satisfaction. Canute and his followers couldn't read the message, because there wasn't one, and what poor bewildered Charlie, now plodding along the horses' tracks, would think of it was subject for quiet merriment.

The aborigines in their camp, and Charlie on the tramp, would most certainly be perturbed by the signals they couldn't understand.

Aided by memory of the wall map in Wootton's office, Bony estimated he was then nine miles direct from Mount Eden homestead. That the smokes would be seen by the aborigines there, he was confident, and that Canute would dispatch some of his bucks to investigate would be certain.

An hour later he was riding up one of the gibber-armoured slopes over which Arnold had to pass to reach the old homestead for the iron, and on arriving at the summit of a tabletop he was amused and gratified to see smokes going up from Canute's camp.

He was about to begin the long descent to a wide belt of

trees and a windmill, when he saw an answering signal rising from the place at which he had created both diversion and confusion. Charlie was informing Canute that a debil-debil was playing hell in general.

Throughout the night, Bony sat with his back against a tree some three hundred yards from the rock-hole near which was based Yorky's camp. He waited for Charlie, but Charlie failed to materialize from the encircling darkness.

THIRTEEN

BALANCING RESULTS

S I G N S O F wind were not disturbing until noon the next day, when the sky was streakily washed with slacked lime and the sun's rays were tinged with red. Bony rode a hundred yards from the fence to accept the meagre shade of a patch of bull-oaks which, when first seen, appeared to be ten miles distant when actually they were within a mile, and looked to be thriving British oaks on a mountain top when they were half dead on the slope of a shallow rise.

The flies were in festive mood. Slightly smaller than the common house fly, Bony had kept them at bay with a leafy switch, like a pasha riding a small donkey, and now they followed him into the shade, to attack again as he removed the saddles from the tormented horses, not bothering to tether them as they were not so stupid as to wander into the sunglare. At once they sought his company, when he, having made a small fire to boil water, found refuge in the rising heated air that he might convey food to his mouth, and the horses stood either side of him, their heads also in the hot air. Better the heat than flies drowning in the eyes.

Of Charlie he had seen nothing since the morning of yesterday, and so far nothing resulted from his trick smoke-signalling. He had observed no puzzling tracks, and since leaving Mount Eden homestead had found no sign of Ole Fren Yorky.

Still, in this country, the wise do not hasten to peer beyond the crest of a sand dune, but rather await the dune to come to them. And it indicated its intention of so doing when, later this day, Bony was continuing his journey along the endless boundary fence.

He and the fence were crossing a vast area of gibbers. Fortunately he was proceeding eastward, because it was impossible to see anything westward for the glare of reflected light from the ironstone armour covering the ground. Ahead some few miles, the fence would terminate at Lake Eyre, seventeen miles south of the Mount Eden homestead.

He saw the first of the smokes rising west of north, and so distant that they looked like gold straws sprouting from the mirage. There were three. One was continuous, one was broken at long intervals, and the third broken at short intervals. They lasted for about ten minutes and ended in a flat-top of dark-grey fog. Then four smokes rose from near or at Canute's camp. Two were unbroken.

That was all, this day, and when night masked the heated earth, and Bony hadn't reached Yorky's next water-camp, he hitched his horses to scrub trees, sat with his back to another, and dozed fitfully until the first ray of dawn.

Before the sun rose, during those magic moments when this Earth is pure and without deceit, smokes rose from Canute's camp, from far to the west, far to the south, and far beyond Mount Eden's northern limits.

As Bony rode, a grim little smile puckered his firm mouth, and he said to the horse: 'When everyone even remotely concerned in a crime sits down, then do something to make them stand. My smokes have certainly made someone stand.'

Before noon he came to a bore languidly spouting water on the far side of the fence, and remembered having camped here when journeying to Mount Eden. Passing through a gateway, he watered the horses and was filling the drums when he heard on the Mount Eden side of the fence a succession of shots sounding like rifle reports produced by a stock-whip. Minutes passed, then he saw the rider cantering to the gateway. He rode through to Bony's camp fire, vaulting off the animal before it stopped.

'Day-ee, Inspector. How you doing?' asked Harry Lawton.

'So-so,' replied Bony. 'Have a spot of tea?'

'My word.'

Young Lawton unstrapped the quart pot from his saddle, removed the cup-lid and filled it from Bony's billy. He raised the cup and said:

'Good hunting! Flamin' hot, isn't it? Going to blow like

hell before night by the look of that sky.'

The brown eyes bespoke casual curiosity. The shaven face, the neck and chest revealed by the open shirt and the bare forearms had the smooth firmness of flesh possessed by Charlie, and were almost the same colour. Lawton's trousers were of grey gabardine, his riding boots of quality kangaroo hide, and his spurs were goosenecked and fitted with sixpences to make them jingle. He displayed the art of sitting on his heels without sitting on the spurs.

'What are you doing out this way?' asked Bony.

'Me? Oh, riding the ruddy fence and turning the cattle back towards the homestead. Cattle will hang around trying to get to the water this side of the boundary. You been missing some fun.'

'Oh!'

'My word!' Lawton grinned. 'Been hell and low water down at the abos' camp. Best riot come ever. You oughta see some of 'em. Rex is dragging an ear over his shoulder, Sarah's lost half her teeth somewhere. Meena got hanks of her hair pulled out, and somebody wielded a waddy against old Murtee and outed him.'

'When did all this happen?' sharply inquired Bony.

'Night before last. Heck of a good go. We seen only the tail end of it. Bodies lying all over the joint when me and the boss and Arnold got there. Crikey! If only I had a movie camera. Been thinking a long time of getting one.'

'You pacified them?'

'Pacified 'em!' Lawton broke into a guffaw. 'Strike me green, they was all pacified enough. Round about eight we heard the roarin' and screamin'. Boss came over from the house, but we told him to let 'em alone. He wanted to pacify 'em as you call it. Arnold said they'd quieten down by the time we wanted to sleep, and we were arguing about it when Meena came tearing up to say if something wasn't done there'd be killings for sure.

'So we went along. Would have toted our guns, but Wootton wouldn't have it. Said we didn't want shot abos lying around. Like I told you, there was plenty of abos lying around, but they wasn't shot. You'd have laughed when we got the camp fire blazing for light. Kids screaming; lubras yelling; abos shouting dirt and abos crawling round looking for waddies and things they'd dropped.

'There was old Canute rollin' about, and when I asked him what he thought he was doing in his dungeon he tells me that a Kurdaitcha knocked him down. Feller called Jimmy Wall Eye thought he'd start something and made a lash at Arnold. You should have seen it. It was a beaut. Arnold prodded him on his good eye, and that fixed him.'

'But what was it all about?' asked the unsmiling Bony, and Harry Lawton laughed again and said no one knew or would tell. He went on:

'Next morning, the boss sent Arnold to the camp with the truck. Sent me with him. Said we had to gather up all the wounded and take 'em in to Doc Crouch to patch up. But there ain't no wounded, no abos at all. They'd all cleared out except Sarah and Meena. They're back on the job cookin' and what not. Hell! I'll have to get that camera. How Rex is goin' to get his ear back on I can't see.'

Lawton stowed his lunch-cloth into a saddle-bag, and the quart pot he strapped to the saddle, then, standing loosely beside Bony and rolling a cigarette, he said:

'Reckon I'll be pushing off. Which way you makin'? Along to Yorky's Lake camp?'

'Yes. How far from here?'

' 'Bout six miles. Bit of horse-feed about the place, but crook in a dust-storm. You doing any good mooching about?'

'Not much,' admitted Bony.

'D'you know what I reckon, Inspector? I reckon Yorky ditched the kid in a sandhill, and got for his life over to the railway and jumped a train for the Alice. Easy done, y'know. Me and a mate jumped the rattler out of Loaders and put in a week up there on a bender, then jumped her back again to Loaders. Well, be seein' you.'

Harry Lawton didn't mount that horse. He rose up and into the saddle. He did not dismount to open the gate and close it when passing into Mount Eden country; he did that chore from the saddle. Then he waved and cantered into the mirage, which made him look like an ant on a grasshopper. And, automatically, Bony gathered his lunch equipment.

The fracas at the aborigines' camp disturbed him because he was sure the cause did not lie in his signals, but in that absence of Charlie and Meena for which they had not given adequate account. That Wootton had sent a truck to take the injured to Loaders Springs indicated the seriousness of the fighting.

Meanwhile there was yet one more of Yorky's camps to inspect, and if this provided no clue to the mystery of his whereabouts, the possibility of his having escaped from this vast Lake Eyre Basin was a strong probability. Again riding along the Mount Eden side of the boundary fence, he went back over the visit of Harry Lawton, and his own impressions.

There are many Harry Lawtons in the bush country proper, even in these days when Australian youth heads for safe government jobs. The spirit of adventure burns brightly in the Lawtons and they are free of the herd instinct.

Debonair youth! The spurs, the wide felt hat, the open shirt, the belt holding the array of small pouches, including a holstered revolver, the delight in the long stock-whip having a bright green silk cracker to produce loud reports, ranging from slow rifle fire to the rat-tat-tat of a machine-gun, all told the story of zestful youth.

Harry Lawton could have started the uproar at the aborigines' camp, where there were several maidens verging on womanhood. From what Pierce had said, Harry Lawton would accept cheerfully many defeats if balanced by a few triumphs. But the odds were in favour of the cause lying in Charlie and Meena and the suspected association with Inspector Bonaparte.

The first wind gust reached Bony about two o'clock. The sun was then distinctly yellow atop a canopy of light grey haze. Instead of the willi-willies, growing clouds of red dust rolled over the land, and on coming to the 'coast' dunes Bony found all the crests smoking fitfully, as though the storm was stoking fires below. The fence began to switch-back over ranges of sand, so that on coming to the summit of a range he saw down on the flat a dilapidated hut built of corrugated iron, a windmill over a well, and a rickety horse yard.

Having hobbled the horses to wander over to the drinking trough and seek a meal from the deceptively unedible herbage, Bony entered the hut of some ten feet by ten in area. Here again were the iron oil drums in which were rations of flour, tea, sugar, matches and tobacco, tinned meat and fish. Here again were oddments of ropes. On a bench-table was a hurricane lamp, and in a corner opposite the open fireplace a tin of kerosene. All the ordinary possessions of an ordinary bushman, save that this bushman named Yorky suffered no losses from wandering aborigines.

The strengthening wind had already made the hut's iron sheets give tongue, but the dim interior was entirely free of the tormenting flies, and gave instant relief from the compelling omniscience of limitless space. Bony brought his gear inside and dumped it on the single bunk, and made a fire for a brew of tea; for no sensible man will drink unboiled water if he can ignite a flame and has tea in his kit, and so reduce the danger of stomach trouble.

Presently, sitting on a case at the bench-table, and sipping scalding hot tea, he smoked cigarettes and worked at his ledger, trying to balance efforts with results.

Was Yorky holed up inside or outside this station boundary fence? Facts could not be ignored. Inside the boundary of Mount Eden were camps at a water supply, and containing food stores. Outside was nothing but waterless aridity, save in the deep holes in the bed of the Neales River, and that was fifty miles away, and in country where even the aborigines on walkabout starved. The answer was certainly not to be found by riding haphazardly hither and yon.

A less patient man would have despaired at Bony's accountancy.

FOURTEEN

THE FUGITIVE'S STORY

THE BOUNDARY fence at this end, like that north of the homestead, terminated far out into the mud of the lake, and beyond the efficient barrier a line of old posts told of past years when the mud had been harder and the fence needed additional extension.

Bony sat on the shore-dune and looked at Lake Eyre. He was unable to recall anything more depressing than this vast plain of dark mud fading into the opaque vacuum of neither earth nor sky. This late afternoon there was nothing of the glamorous magic created by the mirage, nothing to break the flat monotony which brought him abruptly to question his sanity for sitting there and looking at it. Even the dunes were more interesting. They, at least, were actively shedding their headgear of sand and building elsewhere.

What at first he thought was a crow only gradually commanded full attention. The object was a long way out over the mud, and moved in a brownish haze. It wasn't hopping like a bird, or walking like one, and minutes later it took size and shape to reveal itself as a dog.

Obviously it was a wild dog, but what it was doing there was not obvious.

Salt! Was that the answer? It might be, because there was no evidence of salt in Bony's range. That it was a dingo was practically certain, and wild animals will often travel extraordinary distances and to extraordinary places for salt. Still intrigued, Bony realized suddenly that the sun had gone down, and he was conscious of the rising wind removing sand from under him, so that he was sitting deeper and deeper into the dune. The dog, the lake, the world could go hang this evil evening which night would blessedly banish, and he tramped down the dune to the flat where was the hut.

There wasn't much of a wood supply, so he gathered sticks and dead roots as he progressed, and among the debris he picked up was a piece of board. The load he dumped beside the hearth, then made sure the lamp was full, and lit the wick. His fire was out and he built another, and then he strapped the bells to the necks of the horses, and shortened their hobble chains. The final chores done, he was returning to the hut when the wind brought to him a man's sobbing cry.

On the crest of landward dune stood an aborigine. He was naked save for shorts. He carried no weapon. Standing there, his legs to the knees were almost obliterated by the flying sand-mist. Then he collapsed and plunged head-first down the steep slope, his body riding in an avalanche of sand.

He was trying to stand when Bony reached him.

'Why the hurry, Charlie? What's the matter?'

There was caked blood on the left side of Charlie's head, and splotched over his right shoulder. His eyes were glazed with fatigue, and now his legs were useless. Exerting tremendous effort, he managed to emit a sound like the word 'hut'. Wrapping one of Charlie's arms about his neck, Bony half dragged and half carried him to the hut, where he dumped him on the bunk, and stood in the doorway expecting to see enemies cresting the sand ridge over which Charlie had come.

No one, nothing, appeared. The wind brought the tinkle of the horse bells telling that they were feeding undisturbed. Behind him the rasping of the aborigine's breathing was gradually diminishing, and he slammed the door and wedged it with the piece of case board. Then he fed Charlie water, a tablespoon of it, at long intervals.

For an aborigine to be so knocked out indicated how stern the chase had been, how relentless the pursuers. The pounding chest slowly ceased its labouring, and then came a succession of long sighs, and finally Charlie tried to sit up, and was pushed down.

'So the abos are after you,' said Bony.

'Yair. Wild fellers. Ole Canute brought 'em. Smoked for 'em. They nearly got me, and I'd already had enough in a brawl in our own camp.'

'Calm down, Charlie,' Bony urged. 'All safe here with me. I'll get the billy going, and we'll eat, and then we'll talk. Head ache?'

'Like hell.'

'They try to spear you?'

'Tossed a couple at me.'

'They *must* be annoyed.' Bony slung the billycan on the hook over the fire, then dug into a saddle-bag for aspirin, and cartridges for the automatic. Fortunately, the iron hut wouldn't burn, and the iron was in fairly good condition. There was the point that the aborigines' spears could be driven through the iron, but this he doubted as he knew of no precedent. Giving Charlie two tablets and a small amount of water, he said:

'Met Harry Lawton today. He told me there had been a fight in the camp night before last. Is that where your head was injured?'

'Crack on the head in that fight. Shoulder gashed by a spear when it whanged past me.'

'Close as all that, eh? Must be serious. These wild fellers, where did they come from?'

'Other side of the Neales. They must have travelled fast to of got down here in the time. First thing I know of 'em, I'm having a drink at the bore where you met Harry. Four of 'em. I cleared out fast.'

'You were still on my tracks?'

'Yair.'

'How come you were in the camp when the fight took place? You were not on my tracks then.'

Charlie sat up despite Bony's motion to lie still. His scalp was opened and would need stitching, and the sight of the wound recalled Bony to having seen somewhere in the hut a packing needle and twine. The shoulder wound looked less ugly, but had bled much, and the final tumble down the dune, having added sand to perspiration, completed a picture of sufficient grotesqueness to make a man laugh – or shudder. Charlie rolled a cigarette, and Bony lit it for him, and waited for the reply to his last question.

'Your bloody smokes started it,' mumbled Charlie, 'I was keeping well back, like you said, when I seen 'em going up, and 'cos they was in line I couldn't read 'em, but I knew they was sent for Canute. They sort of stonkered me.' The whites of Charlie's eyes betrayed the inherent fear of the inexplicable, and explained his following actions. 'So I sit down and wait to see Canute's smokes, and when none came, I worked it out I ought to go back to the camp and find out what to do.'

Now the eyes gleamed, and the nostrils flared.

'I got back when Canute and Murtee and the Old Men were having a palaver, and the first thing Murtee says to me is about the tracks we left at the bore camp the night before. That Canute, he's a cunnin' old bastard. He got to know about Meena tracking me, and he sent young Wantee off tracking her. And Wantee told him all about us camping with you.

'They had Meena hobbled to a tree with a bit of old rope, and Murtee tells me they goin' to knock her on one knee to make out it's an accident, instead of smashing both knees 'cos Pierce would be a wake up. And while they're tellin' me, I seen a tomahawk biting into a tree, and I grabbed it out and ran to Meena, and she seen me coming and put her leg over the tree root, so's I could chop the rope off her with one hit.'

Charlie was re-living the scene. The nerves of his face were jumping, making his eyes roll, and his mouth was wide and grinning. His arms illustrated the description of what followed.

'There's Murtee yellin' to the mob to get me, and all I got's a tomahawk. They don't like that, and knows I'd of sunk it anywhere I could. I'm ready for 'em, and then the next thing happened was Sarah. That Sarah! Seems they'd tied her up to a tree too, and Meena got her loose.' Charlie laughed. His voice rose to excited shouting. 'Sarah, she's got a tree all to herself, and she wops it against Murtee's head like she's Ma Kettle and Murtee don't argue. Then the mob is on to me. Rex is lookin' for it, and I'm decidin' where I'll bury the tomahawk in him, when Meena gets between and goes to blind him with her fingernails. Anyway, I gets in a smack with the flat of the blade, rememberin' just in time that Rex and me is mates. And out goes Rex.

'There's old Canute yelling what to do, and the mob's getting close to him, and me in the middle. I can hear that dirty black bastard tellin' 'em not to kill us, and then I gets a wallop on me head and I'm out. Next thing I see is Sarah standing on Canute's belly. Then she jumps up and down on it, and Canute don't do any more yelling. I see Rex up on his feet and he's bashin' young Whistler who's tearing out Meena's hair, and after that what come in front went down, and I had a waddy instead of the tomahawk, and I don't know how. Anyway, they're going down as they comes up, and suddenly there's not so many, and it's getting dark after a couple of 'em sort of rolls over the fire.

'After a bit the truck come with the boss and Arnold and the others. We're all stonkered by now, but that fool Jimmy Wall Eye makes a swipe at Arnold and Arnold woodens him. That finishes the deal, and after finding there's no one dead, but a lot of 'em still sleeping, they go off back to the homestead, takin' Sarah and Meena with 'em.

'Next mornin' we all clear out. You know how it is, Inspector. All the lubras get the young gum leaves and mash 'em with their teeth, so's they have a mouthful of pap, and they push the stuff into cuts and wounds and plaster Lake mud over the lot. Canute, or someone, tells 'em to leave me alone. I can go to hell, and think I'd better go bush while things cool down. Think best I can do is to go back to trackin' you, and I'm doin' this when I see Canute's smokes and the smokes what the wild blacks sent up. Canute called for a corroboree, but the next thing was them wild fellers coming at me at the bore. They'll be around somewhere now.'

'A good fight, eh?' dryly commented Bony, and Charlie grinned.

'You're tellin' me. That Sarah! Heavy as a ridin' hack. And both feet up in the air and down on Canute's belly.'

'And she used a tree as a waddy?' Bony chuckled.

'Musta pulled it out of the ground, a dead stump ten feet long,' shouted Charlie. 'That Sarah!'

'And Meena really enjoyed it?' pressed the delighted Bony.

'I'll say. That Meena! That Meena!' Charlie rocked with ecstasy of the memory. 'You should of . . .'

The hut wall received a terrific blow and cut short the story. In the ensuing silence both men froze against the backdrop of the wind, and at a distance a guttural halting voice shouted:

'You come out, you Charlie feller. Big-feller policeman, you stop there. You all right.'

Bony aimed his pistol in the direction of the voice and sent a bullet through the iron. There were no more shouted instructions. Even the wild blacks would know better than to attack openly a representative of the white man's law. Could they lay hands on Charlie, he would disappear and never be found.

They dined off Yorky's tinned herrings in tomato sauce, and drank much tea heavily laced with sugar, and then Bony suggested treating Charlie's wounds.

'They're all right,' laughed Charlie as though it were a joke. 'They'll keep.'

'Don't argue,' snapped Bony. 'You must have the scalp stitched up. Can't go on looking like that. Make Meena sick.'

'That Meena! You reckon so?'

'I certainly do. I've got some salve. Let's see if Yorky has any antiseptic.'

They poked about, and Charlie came up with a can of tar.

'Here yar. Heat her up and it'll do. Sew me up like a camel. Okee?'

'You'd get me into jail for cruelty to dumb animals. No. Best thing is kerosene. I've a hold-all in this bag with some strong thread.'

The wound was ugly to behold. Bony persuaded Charlie to sit on a case with his face in his hands to protect his eyes, his elbows on his knees. The parted scalp was lacerated along the edges, glued to the skull with sand, and at least four inches long. Water inside the hut was now limited to a couple of pints, and it was a long time until day broke, when, Bony was confident, he could go to the well.

Fortunately for Charlie, the hold-all contained a couple of darning needles, and, having threaded these, Bony dropped them and the thread into a tin containing kerosene. To distract the patient's attention, he mentioned having seen the dingo out on the mud.

'Funny thing about them dingoes,' Charlie said, not flinching as Bony sponged the open wound with kerosene. 'Reckon they go right across the lake to the other side. I seen a bitch with her pups once. They were coming in, the old gal and four beaut pups. Looked gold in the early mornin'. You know, like four baby suns and one big one. I watched 'em. Seen the pups was keeping close to the mother, and d'you know why?'

'Why?' said Bony fitting a piece of leather into the palm of his hand to drive the needle. 'This is going to hurt me more than it will hurt you,' he thought, but didn't say.

'They was followin' a pad,' replied Charlie, and moved not a fraction as the needle pierced the lip of the parted scalp. 'Them dingoes know their way across. They follow their own roads across the mud. The pups was keepin' close so's not to muddy their feet. I could see the track they was following. I went down to the dog pad and walked out a bit to meet the dingo and her pups and see what they do. And they just turned round and went out again, still following the pad. How's the sewing?'

'Halfway through,' encouraged Bony. 'How old would you say the pups were?'

' 'Bout five weeks, might be six.'

'She couldn't have brought them across the lake from the other side. She must have taken them out from your side for a walk?'

'Don't think. She didn't go out on the pad she was coming in on. No fresh tracks telling it, anyway.'

'How far did you go out on the path?'

'Couple of hundred feet. Could have gone a bit more, but I knew I wouldn't catch up with them pups.'

'Many such pads?'

'No. That one's half a mile this side of the homestead.'

'Interesting,' drawled Bony. 'Well, the job's done. Here's a rag to wipe your eyes clear. You'll have to get someone to cut the stitches in about a week, if you're not dead from tetanus.'

FIFTEEN

BOARDS AND DINGO ROADS

THE WIND clawed the iron roof and now and then shook even the walls. The two men slept fitfully, Charlie tautened by the proximity of the wild aborigines outside, and Bony beset by recent events, plus the need for sleep in a comfortable bed.

Eventually morning came, to reveal several holes in the roof, and crevices about the door frame and under the eaves.

By standing on a case or the bunk, Bony was able to survey the surrounding scene. The wind continued high but had moved to the south, was noticeably cool, and no longer possessed the power to lift dust and move sand dunes. There was no sign of Charlie's pursuers.

'I'll fetch water,' said Bony. 'Let me out and wedge the door until I return.'

He picked up a petrol tin bucket, thrust cartridges into a pocket and the automatic into another, and removed the wedge. The door swung inward. His hand was moving towards Charlie, in the act of tossing the board to him, when a projecting piece of metal halted the movement.

The board was about two feet long, and seven or eight inches wide. One end was curved to a blunt point, and the original sharp edge along one side had been rasped to smoothness. Across the width and at about one-third from the square end was screwed a wooden cleat, and at equidistance from both ends holes had been bored close to the edge of both sides.

Setting down the bucket, Bony examined the board more closely, and failed to discern its use since it had formed part of a packing-case. 'Charlie,' he called, 'what do you make of this? Part of a camel saddle, or what?'

On looking up at the aborigine, he found him staring at a point above his head, his face registering expression of dawning comprehension. Only for a moment was reaction to the board evident, then it gave place to one of vacuity, and the shutters fell behind the black eyes.

'Dunno, Inspector Bonaparte,' replied Charlie, the title and surname slipping into the reply unnecessarily. 'Bit of ole wood belonging Yorky, looks like.'

'Obviously, as it's Yorky's camp. Seen anything like it before?'

Charlie shook his head, and Bony again picked up the bucket, motioned to the opened door, passed outside and heard the door being wedged again.

It was not a time for cogitation. The barren dunes could sprout black figures and discharge a flight of spears. From behind five or six tough mulga trees could step other black men, each with a spear ready to throw. Without haste, or caution, Bony walked the hundred yards to the windmill over the well, where he released the brake to set the mill working to raise fresh water. Casually he leaned against one of the iron legs and scanned the wind-swept, arid surroundings about the mill and the hut. Nothing human appeared, to relieve the depressing scene.

He carried the filled bucket to the hut, and when Charlie opened the door the change of wind proved that the wide iron chimney could smoke.

'Are you firing the place?' Bony asked. And Charlie laughed too loudly before explaining that the fire wasn't properly blazing. He had started it with brush, and, as he spoke, it burst into flame.

'No blackfellers outside,' Bony told him. 'Looks like they cleared out.'

'Too right. They don't like fight with big-feller policeman. Could be they tell Canute to do his own dirty work, the black bastard. What'll we do now?'

'Use that basin to wash in, have a shave, push on to the homestead. We'll follow the beach, to reduce chances of ambush. And you'll be staying close to the homestead while I argue it out with Canute.'

Charlie was decidedly relieved by Bony's cheerfulness. He

103

tossed the case board into the fire, added more fuel to surround the billy with flame, and within thirty minutes they had eaten breakfast, rolled cigarettes, and Bony had brought in the horses. To add importance to the big-feller policeman for unseen eyes, assuming the wild men were watching, they moved off with Charlie haltered by a length of camel nose-line and walking beside Bony's hack as though a prisoner of the Law, white man's ruddy law.

Even Charlie, so close to the primitive, so close to 'nature', failed to sense any nearness of warlike aborigines. As the sun lifted from the horizon, the wind weakened to become a gentle breeze, and the flies kept to the shelter provided by the horses. At noon all the magic of this Earth achieved by the mirage had banished the ugliness of the previous day.

Now and then Charlie chatted, but mostly he walked silently, repeatedly glancing to the rear and even more often directing his gaze to left-ahead, at the shore line of the dunes. Morning passed. A fire and tea and tinned meat separated the morning from the afternoon, and two hours later they sighted the line of pine trees marking the position of the homestead.

'What about the dog pad you were going to show me, Charlie?' asked Bony, and Charlie chuckled and said it was three miles farther on.

Why had the shutters fallen behind his eyes when asked about that case board? Why the dawn of comprehension which had preceded the shutters? What had that board told this aborigine? That the board had brought his mind to understand what he hadn't understood was amply proved. The trick of shuttering the mind without closing the eyes was ever annoying to the questioner, because it was a more emphatic refusal to answer a question than any words could be.

It was but a few nights back that under Bony's questioning Meena had admitted that she did not know where Yorky and the child were, but when asked if she thought Canute knew, down came the shutters. Charlie had betrayed the same reaction, therefore it seemed that neither knew where Yorky was, but believed that Canute did. The board told Charlie a story, but Charlie dropped the shutters on that story.

The subject was occupying Bony's mind when Charlie, still wearing the loop of light rope about his neck, called his attention to the dingo road. From the elevation of the back of his horse, Bony could see it, a thin winding ribbon slightly darker than the bordering mud, and extending to infinity. Dismounting, he strode to the junction of the pad with the beach, and could see the tracks of dogs going out and coming in. On the cement-hard beach were many marks made by dogs coming off the mud to free their paws of it.

Following concentration, Bony decided that the number of dogs was small, but that the age of the pad was old. The dog traffic had depressed the pad half an inch below the general surface, and when Bony stepped on to it, he found it decidedly harder than outside it.

'A good place to set a dog trap,' he told Charlie, and at this suggestion Charlie laughed, and spuriously joked that the dingoes hadn't harmed any white feller, so why trap him? Bony walked on out, and found that the mud wasn't soft till he had proceeded fifty odd feet. It was certainly a poser, why the dogs went out into Lake Eyre, and the answer couldn't be salt, as salt patches lay quite close to the shore.

Again Bony mounted, and they left the beach and skirted the slope leading to the pines and the homestead gate beyond, which crossed the yards. Bony removed the rope from Charlie and they unsaddled.

'Let the horses go, Charlie, and then take my swag and the bags to the house veranda,' Bony instructed. 'And remember, you are not to leave the homestead until I give word. I'll speak to Mr Wootton about you staying here and doing odd jobs, and then we'll have a good look at that head and decide whether it will do, or if it's a case for the doctor.'

'You fix up with Canute?' asked Charlie, anxiously.

'I'll fix him, Charlie.'

He found Wootton on the east veranda, and the cattleman was obviously freed from a load.

'Bonaparte! Glad you got back. We've had trouble here, as young Lawton told you. He said he'd found you at Number 91 Bore yesterday.'

'Yes. He was quite excited by the brawl at the camp. Said the abos had cleared out.'

'They did, but they came back today. I've kept Meena and her mother here for safety's sake. Got in touch with Pierce, and he treated the affair very casually, I thought. Said the blacks often went to market, and that he never interfered unless to stop a feud, or a killing. When I told him there might be a killing as a result, he asked where you were, then said to give you a couple of days more before he'd move.'

'No one is dead?' mildly asked Bony.

'Don't think so. A lubra came this morning to ask for some pain-killer for Murtee, but I couldn't get anything from her about the rest. I never saw the like of it. They were lying about the camp, some unconscious, many of them bleeding, and all the children in bunches and yelling like mad. And here's Meena. Look at her! Just look at her!'

The girl came forward and placed the tray of afternoon tea on a low table. As she again wore a black dress and white pleated apron, the observer had to go to the top of her head to find anything at odds with this smartly dressed maid. She looked at Bony at first shyly, and then with laughter in her eyes, and Wootton said:

'Show him, Meena.'

She bent forward to permit Bony to view the linen pad marking where she had lost a patch of hair by violent extraction, and Bony chuckled, saying:

'Not as bad as Charlie, Meena. Have you seen him yet?'

'That Charlie!' Meena laughed. 'Charlie says that ole black bastard sent the wild blacks after him.'

'Meena!' expostulated Wootton. 'You must not refer to anyone like that. What do you mean, sending the wild abos after Charlie?'

'I will explain that,' Bony interposed. 'You, Meena, make Charlie take a shower and then look at his scalp and tell me what you and Sarah think should be done for it.'

'First pour the tea,' ordered Wootton. 'Inspector Bonaparte must be tired and thirsty.'

This she did, expertly, gravely, and when she had gone the cattleman exploded.

'Don't understand it, damned if I do. Look at her, clean as a new pin. Her clothes are right, excepting those red shoes. Speaks all right, too. Any city woman would give thanks for such a maid. And then what? A half naked Amazon clawing, punching, kicking, screaming and biting.'

'And thoroughly enjoying herself.'

'Without a doubt. Curious way to enjoy oneself. I saw a man with his ear almost torn off. And Sarah, our cook, brandishing a log of wood as big as a tree. Then there's Charlie. What happened to him?'

'Someone dropped a brick on his head. Opened his scalp. I sewed it up last night. Don't worry about the aborigines, I'll deal with them. By the way, I'm low in tobacco. Can you let me have five or ten pounds in quarter-pound plugs?'

'Of course. But five . . . ten . . .'

'I'd like to borrow your car or a truck to run along to the camp for an hour. After, of course, we have eaten all these delicious scones baked for us!'

SIXTEEN

BONY BUYS A WOMAN

WANDIRNA, CHIEF of the Orrabunna Nation, alias
Canute, ordered a eucalyptus bath. He was feeling unwell,
what with the rheumatism and the pounding of Sarah's feet
on his stomach, and felt the need for the cure invented by his
ancestors long before the original King Canute played the fool
with his nobles.

The lubras had brought back from their temporary exile
masses of young gum tips, and with these they lined a shallow
grave which had been heated by burning wood. Water was
sprinkled on the gum leaves and through to the earth, which at
once emitted clouds of steam. Finally, when the temperature
had cooled slightly and the heated leaves had become sodden,
a lubra escorted King Canute and invited him to step down
into the grave.

He lay there at full length; a short, fat, white-haired old
man, entirely naked save for the ragged beard covering the
upper portion of his chest. Steam laden with eucalyptus oils,
strong enough to asphyxiate a steer, rose from the interred,
who huffed and grunted and snorted, but stuck it out. The
temperature then falling slowly, the victim gave a stifled
order, and the lubra placed gum branches over the grave to
seal the healing elixir.

Canute, who was now feeling wonderfully soothed, ventured
to stretch one leg and then the other, then his arms, and rejoiced that all the nagging pains were no longer tying knots
with his muscles. Ah! It was good to be a king. He yelled for
the lubras to help him out.

Nothing happened. The lubras were deaf or something. He
shouted again. There must be a lubra to remove the top
branches and hold in readiness for his hot and rejuvenated
body a military overcoat supplied by the Protector of Abo-

rigines. He was not fool enough to stand and meet the chill air of late afternoon.

'Ah!' The branches were being removed, those over his feet first. The outside air told him this. Then, instead of his lubra's voice, he heard another he had remembered.

'Get out, Canute.'

With the suppleness of youth, the King arose and stepped from the grave ... into the military overcoat held ready for him by D. I. Bonaparte. By an arm he was drawn away and urged smartly to the communal camp fire tended by the awed lubras.

'Sit down,' was the next order, and the King subsided on to a tree stump, the heat of the fire scorching his shins and face. Gravely, he was presented with a stick of tobacco and told to chew. He obeyed by halving the tobacco stick with his teeth, and wedging one half into a cheek.

'You tell Murtee come here,' commanded Bony. 'And the Old Men.'

Canute moved the lump from one cheek to the other, and shouted orders. Lubras ran from their jobs, then halted like startled rabbits. Children were hushed, save one small baby lying on an old blanket in company with several others. Men appeared, one after another, and squatted about Canute, and lastly, wearing a mud plaster and looking positively savage, came the Medicine Man. A eucalyptus bath twice as hot might possibly have benefited him too.

From the truck nearby, Bony brought a packing-case and a papered parcel. The parcel he placed on the ground before the semi-circle of aborigines, the case he put over the parcel, and on the case seated himself. Then with slow deliberation he rolled a cigarette, licked it, lit it, and stared at the black eyes watching him with the cold impassivity of iguanas.

Taking up a stick, he drew a tiny circle on the ground at his feet, as though it had to be perfect. Then to the right of the tiny circle he drew, with exaggerated effort, a much larger circle. Done to his pleasing, he spat once into each circle and watched the spittle sink into the sand.

On his throne stump, King Canute chewed vigorously, his

sightless eyes, destroyed by a grass fire, moving slightly as though they could serve the brain behind them. Beside him sat an ancient who looked a thousand years old and probably was not quite ninety. His claw-like hand encircled Canute's wrist. The anthropologists wouldn't believe it, but Bony knew that the Old One was passing what he saw to the mind of the blind man. Thus he had proceeded slowly, and continued so to do.

With his stick Bony indicated the larger circle, saying:

'That is Canute–Wandirna, Head Man of the Orrabunna Nation.' There was sudden relaxation of tension. He pointed to the smaller circle. 'That is all other blackfellers inside one humpy.' His stick passed over the ground as though expunging the circles, returned to the large circle, saying: 'That is big-feller policeman, ME. And this small one is Constable Pierce.'

There was silence while he stared into every pair of black eyes, and held his gaze for a long minute on the eyes of the old man holding Canute's wrist. What the old man saw in his blue eyes, Bony knew Canute was seeing, too. The lubras were silent and still, hunched just beyond the communal fire, and the men and children stood also in packed units. Bony said:

'Long time ago, Sarah promised little baby Meena to Canute. Now Canute is old, and he takes eucalyptus bath and likes tobacco better than young lubras. He likes to sit in the sun and hear happy voices of his people about him, and tell them what the spirits of the Alchuringa would have them do. What do you say, Canute?'

'Big-feller policeman speaks true,' agreed Canute, adding: 'There's blackfeller law and whitefeller law.'

'Canute speaks true,' agreed Bony. 'But whitefeller law more strong than blackfeller law. Still, we palaver now about blackfeller law. Bimeby we palaver about whitefeller law. We talk about Sarah and her Meena she promised to Canute long time ago. Long time ago Meena belong to Canute. All right! Okee! I am sitting on forty plugs of black tobacco, as many as your fingers on both hands make five times. I trade all that tobacco for Meena.'

Silence followed this proposition until Murtee said:

'Meena Orrabunna lubra. You are Worcair man. No can do.'

'I am whitefeller policeman,' countered Bony. 'I say for you to go to jail, you go to jail in Loaders Springs quick and good. I see you Murtee; I can see you. You tell Canute smoke for wildfeller to come play hell on Mount Eden. You break whitefeller law. I big whitefeller policeman. You, Canute feller, forty plugs of tobacco for your Meena, eh?'

The tendons along the skeleton arm of the aborigine, acting as Canute's eyes, tightened when urging acceptance without argument, and Canute said:

'You sit on tobacco?'

'I sit on forty tobacco plugs.'

'I trade okee, all right.'

With his stick, Bony now erased the two circles. Then he drew two very large circles slightly overlapping. He called Meena, and the girl emerged from the car parked just off the track and came to him through the gathered aborigines. She was wearing white shorts, and nothing else save the pad of linen on her head.

She stood inside one of the circles, and into the other circle Bony emptied the plugs of tobacco. The old man urged Canute to rise, and brought him forward to stand chest to chest with Bony where the circles overlapped. Behind Bony was the tobacco; behind Canute stood Meena, Canute's left wrist still grasped by the Counsellor.

Murtee now came forward and gave to Canute a flint, and the King explored Bony's chest with his free hand and nicked the flesh. He passed the flint to Bony, and Bony nicked his chest. Each wetted a fingertip with the other's blood and pressed the finger to the blood on his own chest.

The deal was accomplished. Canute fell on his knees and pawed the tobacco like a miser counting his gold, and Bony caught Meena by a forearm and marched her over to the car, pushed her in, closed the door and returned to the communal fire.

The tobacco had vanished. Everyone, men and women and the older children, were chewing tobacco. Canute was back on

111

his throne. It was some time before King, Grand Vizier and
Counsellors regained their pre-business gravity.

'There is another trade,' Bony told them, 'Blackfeller law
for whitefeller law. What for you all go crook when I send up
smoke telling Worcair feller I am okee, all right? What for
you catch Sarah and Meena? What for you all fight in camp?
You tell me, eh?'

Faces like gargoyles. Eyes blank like shuttered shop windows in a riot. Bony slowly rolled a cigarette, actually making
what looked like a cigarette.

'I tell you, eh? You tell Charlie track along big-feller
policeman. I catch-um Charlie. Then I catch-um Meena.
They don't tell me but I know why you tell Charlie to track
me, see what I do. You tell Charlie to do all that because you
scared I find Yorky and Linda. All right! Whitefeller law say
you all go to jail. You track white policeman. You try to lame
Meena and bash up Charlie. Then you smoke for wildfeller-
blackfeller come along to catch up Charlie, kill Charlie, hide
his body in sand dune, no whitefeller policeman then know
where Charlie is. You say Charlie gone long way away. No
good to whitefeller policeman. You all go jail okee, all right.'

The sun was westering and bars of light gold lay athwart the
scene and illumined the faces of Canute and his Counsellors.
All were distinctly uneasy, obviously recalling the tales of jail
existence told them by Pierce in previous conferences.

'Blackfeller live blackfeller law,' observed Murtee, spitting
tobacco juice towards Bony.

'You live blackfeller law, eh?' Bony said. 'I trade. You all
live whitefeller jail pretty quick. You tell me where Yorky is,
and you no live whitefeller jail. You all trade, eh?'

Eyes lifted from the ground. Men looked at men, and the
lubras frowned, scowled, muttered. Finally all eyes were
directed to the blind Chief. Even Murtee waited on his de-
cision. The minutes passed, and tension increased so that when
Canute stood and the greatcoat, unbuttoned, opened to reveal
his enormous paunch and spindle-stick legs, still there was
proof that the aura of authority can crown an aborigine.

'Yorky is a whitefeller-blackfeller. Blackfeller not trade.'

He sat down on his stump, and instantly Bony said:

'Bimeby blackfeller trade. Bimeby blackfeller trade in whitefeller jail. You forget about Sarah, about that fight. Anything you do to Sarah, you all look out. Anything you do to Charlie, you all look out. You tell wild-blackfeller go back to camp, clear off your country, stay off your country, pretty quick. Palaver finish. Trade finish. Meena my woman. Tobacco your chew. Okee, all right!'

'Okee all right! Meena your woman,' agreed Canute cheerfully, obviously happy that the conference was ended.

Bony stepped forward to prove the proven. He stood before the King of the Orrabunna Nation and held out his hand. The blind man detached his hand from that of the Counsellor and reached forward. They shook hands.

Gravely Bony walked back to the car. Without speaking, he went backward into the seat behind the wheel and drove on towards Loaders Springs. Meena was puzzled, waiting for him to speak. For fifteen minutes Bony drove and then stopped.

He made two cigarettes, one of which he gave to the girl and then he said:

'You belong to me. I bought you with five pounds of tobacco. What Marie, my wife, is going to say doesn't bear thinking about.'

'Don't tell her.'

'You don't know why I bought you, do you?'

'Of course I do. You bought me because you desire me.'

'Don't be silly,' Bony said, severely.

'Silly! What's silly about it? A man doesn't buy a lubra unless he wants her.'

'Or something else from her, Meena. You are my woman, remember. So you will tell me what I want to know. The other night I asked you a question. I asked you if you knew where Yorky is holing up, and you said you didn't know. Do you know?'

'No, I don't,' replied Meena angrily.

'I asked also if Canute knew where Yorky is, and you would not say. I ask you now if Canute knows. Tell me.'

Meena tossed the cigarette end beyond the open window,

113

tossed her hair without regard to the pad, and sulked. Bony partially turned and slowly rubbed the palms of his hands together.

'These can hurt more than a waddy,' he said. 'You are my woman, as I have told you more than once. What you tell me is no longer any business of Canute, so leave your side of the gulf and meet me.'

'Gulf! What d'you mean, gulf?'

'Never mind. Answer my questions. First, does Canute know where Yorky is?'

'Yes, he does. So does Murtee.'

'Does Charlie know?'

Quickly the girl shook her head.

'But Charlie knows that Canute knows?'

The head nodded.

'What else does Canute know?'

Reluctantly the girl turned to meet his eyes, tears in her own.

'We been trying to find out, Sarah and me. Ole Fren Yorky was always kind to Sarah and me. What for he went and killed Mrs Bell we can't find out. Sarah and me are glad he wasn't caught by Mr Pierce, and if we knew where he was we wouldn't tell you.'

'I'd make you tell me,' snapped Bony.

'No, you wouldn't. Nor make me blackfeller way, either.'

'But what of little Linda Bell? A white child, frightened, perhaps hungry, living like a dingo with Yorky.'

'She'll be all right with Yorky. I know. Yorky is my father. There's no white man good like Yorky.'

Bony sighed.

'There are times when I am a very poor policeman, Meena. I should take you from this car and beat you, and no one could interfere because you are my woman. It is said that your father, for a reason we don't yet know, murdered an inoffensive woman and abducted her small child, and you are in sympathy with him. You don't believe, do you, that Yorky didn't shoot Mrs Bell?'

'I don't know, Inspector, I don't know,' she wailed. 'He

114

must have been mad or something. And now you make me want to help you catch him, and have him sent away and killed. Go on, beat me. I want you to beat me. I'm your woman. You bought me.'

She twisted farther round to bury her face in her arms, and gently Bony twisted his fingers in her short black hair.

The hell fired by the meeting of two races and ever open to receive him, he knew was open to take her, too.

'Would you like me to tell you why I bought you, Meena?'

Abruptly her face lifted, and she was looking at him with tear-washed and grey-flecked eyes.

'I bought you from Canute for Charlie.'

SEVENTEEN

BONY TRADES HIS WOMAN

BONY STOOD before the open french window of his bedroom and regarded the rising slope topped by the pine trees, and the slope was the rock he had not yet cracked although he had chipped it; the inscrutable surface of this land he was unable to delve into, although having scratched it.

Were it not for the possibility that the abducted child was alive, he would have enjoyed to the full the tussle with the aboriginal element behind his investigation into the murder of Mrs Bell, would have accepted the hardness of the rock, the imperviousness of the surface, as a test for his patience. What had appeared a long period of effort was actually less than two weeks, during which he had achieved more than Pierce and his half-hundred men had done in a month.

Now he would hammer and delve in other places.

Donning a gown and slippers, he opened the door and listened for sounds of domestic activity. As anticipated, it was too early for the staff to be at work, and silently he passed along the short passage to the living-room, and crossed to the kitchen.

He was smiling as he primed a kerosene stove with methylated spirits, recalling that he owned a lubra who ought to have been up long since to minister to his thirst, and that, when all was said and established, the Canutes and the Murtees got along very nicely, thank you. The sun about to rise, and the wife still abed! Enough to challenge any aborigine.

He was seated at the kitchen table drinking his third cup of tea and smoking his fifth cigarette, when sounds introduced the cook to her kitchen. Wearing a man's gown she paused a moment to wipe the sleep from her eyes, and then banged the clock on the dresser and ruffled her hair back from her forehead. Still ignoring Bony, she left the kitchen, came back with

116

kindling wood, lit the stove and departed for the outside wash-house.

She reappeared at the same inner door, and this time dressed for the day's toil in a yellow dress, protected by a faded blue apron.

'You are up late,' Bony said.

'Sunday morning,' Sarah countered.

'There's tea in the pot,' he coaxed. 'I'll make you a cigarette.'

She poured tea, brought it to the table and drew up a chair. He could not but note that her forearms were the size of his legs, and regretted he had not witnessed her performance with the tree. He estimated her weight at fifteen stone, and her age still under fifty. On her face were the cicatrices of her totem, and behind her dark eyes the shutters were already lowered to repel his attacks. She accepted the cigarette and evinced surprise when he proffered a light.

Bony sat at ease and regarded her. She came to the point of looking directly at him, and, expecting him to speak, became anxious when he did not. Dark eyes clashed with blue eyes and the table was a gulf between them. A glimmering of the truth met the mind of the primitive woman. This man was not one of her own kind, but, being a woman, her heart was bound to triumph.

'What for you trade Canute for my Meena?' she asked.

'Didn't she tell you?'

Sarah shook her greying head. She had forgotten the tea. The cigarette burned unnoticed between her stumpy fingers. He could see the beginning of anguish creep into her eyes, but he withheld speech, and presently she said:

'What for? You are man from whitefeller country. What for you trade for my Meena? Meena's my Meena. Ole Fren Yorky lie with me. Ole Fren Yorky my man. Ole Fren Yorky marry me blackfeller way. To hell with Mission feller.'

'Better for Meena to be my woman than belong to old Canute,' Bony said. 'What for you promise little Meena baby to him?'

'Long time ago Canute say he tell policeman about Yorky

117

and me, I not promise him baby. I promise him baby then he
still say tell policeman. Yorky little feller. He fight Canute.
Canute no more tell policeman.'

'But he stuck to the promised baby?'

'Yair. She grow up and he try for her. We beat him, we
always beat him. We try beat you, too.'

'You may, but not Meena,' he said, smiling to rouse her.
'Meena, she marry me, big-feller policeman. She go away with
big-feller policeman. You no see Meena no more.'

The large black eyes blazed, and the fire was extinguished
by the blue ice of his own. She began to emit long-drawn sobs,
and down her large face tears fell, reminding him of her
daughter. Her voice now wailed:

'What for Ole Fren Yorky shoot Mrs Bell and run away
with Linda? What for he do that? What for you come and
take my Meena away? What for . . . what for . . . what for . . .'

'How do you know Ole Fren Yorky killed Mrs Bell?' he
demanded. 'You say Ole Fren Yorky run away and Yorky
surely killed Mrs Bell. Other feller p'raps kill Mrs Bell, and
kill Linda and Yorky, too.'

Hope was born like a star and extinguished like a slush
lamp. Sarah's fear and despondency swept back over her.

'They found Yorky's tracks,' she fought back.

'Did you see those tracks?'

'No. Bill Harte did, and Arnold, and Constable Pierce.'

'They ought to know.'

'Yair. Meena and me was put to cooking and housework.
The men went tracking Ole Fren Yorky. They find where Ole
Fren Yorky went to, and wouldn't say anything. Me and
Meena tried to find out.'

'Does Charlie know?'

'Don't think.'

'Did Charlie see Yorky's tracks behind the meat-house?'

'What for he see them? He was put tracking. They all was
that day, soon's the men had their breakfast.'

'Now you listen, Sarah,' he said slowly. 'I tell you something, you promise to keep it secret?'

Slight hesitation, and then surrender. He said:

'Yorky was here last night.'

The statement rocked her before freezing her to immobility.

'You come with me,' he commanded. 'I show you.'

She ambled after him through the back door, along the rear of the house, round to the side veranda on to which his bedroom opened. Opposite his room, steps broke the long veranda railing, and at the bottom of the steps were the imprints of a man who walked on the soles of his feet. The woman halted as though meeting a wall in the dark. She bent low, moved to one side and then the other of the three distinct imprints.

On straightening up, her eyes expressed bafflement, and her voice conviction.

'Them's not Yorky's tracks,' she said.

'Look again.'

She obeyed, shaking her head as again she squinted at the prints from several angles.

'Go fetch Meena. Tell her I want to see her here. Don't tell her about the tracks.'

Meena came in shorts and bath towel. As with her mother, Bony hadn't to indicate the tracks. Like her mother, she stooped and squinted at the prints from different angles. And, like her mother, at first she thought they were Yorky's tracks, and finally decided they were not.

'Yorky here last night?' suggested Bony, and she denied it resolutely. 'All right. Fetch Charlie. Bring him but don't tell him why. You understand?'

'Yes. Someone make believe they are Yorky's tracks?'

'Let us hear what Charlie says.'

Meena dropped the towel and ran like a moorhen to the quarters.

'What for, Mr Bonaparte, what for someone do this?' demanded Sarah, glints in her eyes. 'What for someone make like Yorky came last night?'

'Wait till Charlie's seen them. Even then I mightn't be able to tell you.'

They could see Meena dragging the sleepy Charlie by the hand. She acted fairly when she pushed him forward on reaching the veranda, and Charlie continued under the impetus

119

until he saw the tracks. It was comical how those tracks dashed sleep from his eyes.

'Feller like Yorky,' he said, summing up. 'Walk like Yorky. Don't know that feller.'

They waited upon Bony, and Bony was smiling triumphantly.

'We won't say anything about these tracks being crook ones, eh?'

'If you say so,' agreed Meena. 'But why, who made them?'

'I did. Charlie, could you make them?'

'I'll try.'

'Not now. Back to the kitchen, Sarah, and you, Meena. You're both under the ban of silence. I'll explain to Charlie what I think, and he can tell you. Come on, Charlie.'

They went up the slope, the aborigine in shorts, Bony in flapping dressing-gown. Bony lit a small fire, as blackfellers for centuries have arranged the kindling wood, and motioned Charlie to squat over it with him. With the supreme patience of his race, the aborigine waited while Bony made two cigarettes, and then it wasn't of strange tracks that Bony spoke.

'Meena tell you I traded Canute for her?'

'Yair. Why the hell you do that? You said you'd work on Canute for me.'

'So I did, Charlie. I bought Meena from him. And some time or other I am going to sell her to you.'

For the second time this morning hope was born like a star, but this time it wasn't extinguished.

'I paid forty plugs of tobacco for Meena,' Bony said.

'I pay you more. I got money on the station books.'

'I think Meena is worth five hundred plugs, even a thousand.'

'Tough guy, eh?' charged Charlie, heavily frowning.

'Well, suppose I give you Meena, what would you give me?'

'Anything I got.'

'True answers to my questions?'

'What you want to know?'

'I'm asking would you give true answers to my questions if I give you Meena?'

120

Charlie nodded, and slowly a smile spread over his expressive face.

'It's a deal,' Bony said, and they shook hands over the tiny fire. 'You answer all my questions, I give you Meena. You and Meena go off to the Missioner and be married properly when I say so. Okee?'

'Okee, tough guy.'

'I shall be tough, too. Where is the tribe's treasure house?'

'What! No!'

'All right! No Meena for you.'

Agony filled the black eyes. Sweat broke in great globules on the prominent forehead.

'I can't tell that,' cried Charlie. 'You know I can't tell that.'

'I know where the treasure house is, but I am testing you to be sure you give true answers,' flagrantly lied Bony, and was given the information that the tribe's cherished churinga stones, the magic pointing bones, and all the other relics which chained this tribe of the Orrabunna Nation to the generations of those who had lived and died before them, were in the keeping of a certain tree in a certain place.

'All right, Charlie. Now I know you speak true. Forget about the treasure house. I am your friend; you are my friend. D'you know what plaster of Paris is?' Charlie shook his head.

'Well, do you know what plasticine is?'

'Yair, we worked with that at the Mission.'

'Good! Plaster of Paris is in powder form, and when a little water is mixed with it, it turns to a paste, which dries hard pretty quickly.' Bony made a print of his hand on the ground and illustrated the process of taking casts. 'That day Mrs Bell was shot, Constable Pierce made a plaster cast of the tracks behind the meat-house. I have that plaster cast and from it made the tracks below the veranda steps. So, Charlie, the tracks I made are exactly the same as those which were behind the meat-house. Get me?'

'Yair. Then Yorky's tracks behind the meat-house weren't left by Yorky?'

'That's true. Someone else made those tracks, Charlie, to be sure that a whitefeller would find them. It just happened that no blackfeller saw them. Do you reckon they were good enough to trick Bill Harte and the others?'

Charlie pondered, gravely serious.

'That Bill Harte good bushman,' he said. 'Them tracks pretty good, too. I reckon Bill'd fall for 'em?'

'And the other whitefellers would, too?'

'Yair, quicker than Bill Harte.'

'Now you go down and wait for breakfast. Whisper to Meena that perhaps Yorky didn't shoot Mrs Bell, but is taking the blame for it. Don't tell Meena anything more than that.'

EIGHTEEN

DECISION TO DYNAMITE

THE REACTIONS of Charlie and the women to the prints made with Pierce's plaster cast were identical. They were shocked by seeing what they thought were Yorky's tracks, and astounded by the probability that the original prints declared to have been clear behind the meat-house had been made with a pair of Yorky's old working boots.

Yorky, leaving Mount Eden for a spell at the township, would most certainly leave his working clothes and boots in one of the rooms at the quarters. Thus anyone could use the old boots to make the prints, and smooth out his own tracks as he retreated.

The expert tracker, however, does not limit himself to the actual imprints of the feet. He takes into consideration the angle of each foot from the imaginary dead centre line, as well as the distance separating the prints, revealing the length of the stride, and which leg is shorter than the other.

It is possible for a forger to make exact imprints of a man's boots, but he cannot forge the spaces between the placings of the man's feet accurately enough to deceive an aborigine. The aborigine himself could not make a perfect forgery on all counts.

Constable Pierce, wise man, did not make plaster prints of individual tracks, but had made an extensive cast including two left and one right boot-print, and therefore the prints shown to Charlie and the women were exact replicas of those made behind the meat-house.

Why it happened that no aborigine saw the tracks behind the meat-house could be understood. First Harte had found those tracks. He had taken Arnold to see them, and Eric Maundy. Wootton had seen them, too, but Wootton was no tracker. When Pierce arrived, he was told they were Yorky's tracks, and he saw what he had been led to expect to see. So, the overall acceptance of the forged tracks being genuine, why bother to have them checked by the aborigines urgently needed for the task of tracing Yorky and the child?

Nothing squared in this investigation. It was like a semi-deflated bag, which, when punched, bulged somewhere. The only person who could have no motive for forging those prints was Yorky.

Questions: Who forged them and why? Why, if not to create conviction that Yorky had shot Mrs Bell and taken the child? Instead of one murder, there could be three murders? By the aborigines or the whites?

Bony had waited for the sand dune to come to him. He had prodded a sleeping mystery and it had stirred. He had continued this investigation according to the rules laid down in the practice of crime detection. And now he was convinced that his efforts were being frustrated by a force which the rules had not taken into account. This being so, he showered and dressed in a mood which seldom bothered him.

In the living-room he found Wootton making notes at his radio bench, and the cattleman's mind was busy with the news he had received from a station to the northeast of Lake Eyre.

'Water still pouring into the lake down the Diamantina and Warburton, as well as Coopers Creek,' he said. 'Could be a mighty flood if those rivers continue to run.'

'When did water last flow into the lake?' Bony asked.

'Three years back, but the lake hasn't been properly filled for fifty years, I believe.' Wootton sat and unfolded a napkin. They chose a cereal from the impeccable Meena. 'It would take a hell of a lot of flooding to fill this lake.'

'How do you account for the fact that the shore this side is still moist enough to cover a man's boots with mud, only a short way from the beach?'

'A question I asked a geologist. Pass the sugar, please. Feller called around shortly after I came. Stayed a week. Interesting ideas. Main point seems that a time long ago Lake Eyre was a sea, with hills and dales and holes and things like under other oceans. Then the sea dried out, sort of, leaving the lake still holding water. When that dried out, all the water left was in the holes and things. Get me?'

'Yes. Thank you, Meena. Bacon and eggs, please. Oh, yes, and coffee.'

'Right. The original bottom of the lake is composed of the stuff that forms claypans, like the strip of beach all round. On top of that the wind has blown dust and sand and mullock in which frogs and fish and things have lived and perished, and added their remains. In other words, on the top of the original hard ground there's this thick layer of mud. So what? Meena, I'll have bacon and eggs, too. Well, when the water from the rivers and creeks flows into the lake, it spreads only a little way on the top because most of it seeps down to spread first between the hard bottom and the top mud, as well as having to fill up the deep holes and valleys. So that a heck of a lot of water must flow before the surface of the lake this side shows signs of it, and even then it will appear first under the mud.'

'So that in three years, even longer, without rain, the lake doesn't dry hard even close to shore.'

'That's about the strength of it, Inspector. Meena! Meena! My coffee.'

The girl brought the coffee, and stood behind Bony's chair. She waited for his toast rack to empty, then went to the kitchen for more, making no effort to be so attentive to the cattleman.

'Could I use a horse this morning?' Bony asked. 'Mine is too slow. And I don't want a flash one, either. I have work to do. And I need a sugar sack.'

'Of course. I'll tell Charlie after breakfast. Meena! More toast. What's the matter with you this morning, Meena? Why all the attention to Inspector Bonaparte, and damn little for me?'

Meena apologized, and departed for more toast. Bony said:

'You have not heard that Meena is now my woman?'

'Meena your woman!' Wootton's green eyes opened wide, and he squared his thick shoulders. 'Don't get it.'

'Yesterday afternoon I bought her from Canute.'

'You did! Didn't know he owned her, although someone did

tell me she was promised to Canute when she was a baby. Oh, so that's why you wanted the tobacco. Reckon you got her pretty cheap. What do you think, Meena?'

'Might be too dear, too.'

Mr Wootton's eyes passed over her, from head to red shoes and again to her face. From her he looked at Bony, saying:

'Yes, you bought her cheap. May I ask for what reason?'

'Make a profit on my bargain. Meena, please leave us. I am not going to tell secrets, nor will you.'

The girl came closer, took up Bony's used plate, smiled at Wootton, and almost ran from the room, delaying the giggle which escaped after she entered the kitchen.

'Secrets!' murmured Wootton.

'Lovers' secrets,' Bony said, busy now with a cigarette. 'Tell me. I saw that your fences at one time extended farther into the lake than they do now. How long ago was that?'

'Years before I came here. Could have been when the boundary fence was first built. That was in 1923. I do know that. Many of the original posts still standing. Much of the netting had been renewed. But it's still a good fence. You ride along it?'

'Visited Yorky's old camps. Rations at all of them. D'you keep a check on your rations store?'

'Not a strict one. Why?'

'Sarah hand out much to her tribe?'

'Not that I know of. What's on your mind?'

'I'm wondering what Yorky is living on.'

'Tucker on homesteads over in New South Wales, even across in Western Australia by this time. Surely you don't think he's hanging around Lake Eyre, do you?'

'I have no proof either way. I hope to have it this afternoon. But the footprints behind the meat-house and stated to have been made by Yorky, I have now proved to be forgeries.'

Wootton was obviously astounded.

'Those tracks were not made by Yorky,' Bony went on. 'Three aborigines support that opinion.'

'But everyone, including Pierce, says they were.'

'Did any aborigine see them when they were brought back from the Neales?'

'I don't know. Don't think so. Everything was so rushed. Wait. Pierce had his tracker with him. I did see him looking at the tracks.'

'The police tracker isn't a local abo. He might or might not have noted Yorky's tracks in Loaders Springs. Anyway, he would not be as familiar with Yorky's tracks as the locals.'

Thoughtfully the cattleman loaded his pipe. He said:

'What does that infer?'

'I'm not sure ... yet.' Bony rose. 'Will you have that horse brought in for me?'

'Right away.'

Wootton was decidedly disturbed. Having instructed Charlie, he sat at his office desk for an hour without attending to the litter of documents. It being Sunday there was no smoke-oh for the men, but about ten o'clock Meena came to tell him that tea was made. He went with her to the kitchen, then asked:

'What's all this about the Inspector buying you from Canute?'

The girl smiled demurely, and her mother laughed loudly, but the cattleman could see no joke.

'I suppose you know that the Inspector has a wife where he comes from, and sons almost young men?' he pressed.

Both women laughed, and to neither question would they give answer with words. He was irritated by this evasion, and knew it was futile to be so. He felt that a good deal had happened here on his own territory of which he was ignorant, and that also irritated him. No man likes being a kind of pawn in his own business.

Wootton was again in his office when he heard the thudding of hoofs, guessed that Bony was back, and waited expectantly. A few minutes later Bony entered the office, to put down on the desk the sugar sack he had borrowed. He had taken it away empty; it was now half-filled and tied securely.

Bony asked for sealing wax, and Wootton watched the string knots heavily loaded with wax and sealed with the imprint of a thumb. Then the blue eyes were regarding him seriously.

'The contents of this bag are of value impossible of assessment,' Bony said. 'Could you make room for it in your safe?'

'I think so,' assented Wootton. 'What's in it?'

'I don't wish to sound mysterious, but it would be best for you not to know. Maybe I shall ask you to give it back before tonight. I hope so. Under no circumstances hand it to anyone else, excepting Constable Pierce. He may be here later.'

Wootton took the bag to his safe, rearranging account books and oddments to make room for it. He was further irritated by the secrecy of Bony's sealing wax.

'Would you like to keep the safe key?' he asked with asperity.

'Thanks, but that wouldn't do.' Bony smiled disarmingly.

It was warm inside this room despite the window and door being open. They could hear the low roaring of a willi-willi, and within two seconds a wind rushed on the building as the core of the whirlwind passed behind the men's quarters. The dinner gong, a triangular length of railway iron beaten with an iron bar by the mighty Sarah, broke the tension.

'I have to wash-brush,' Bony said, and left the cattleman to follow more leisurely.

Wootton was already in the living-room when Bony entered to use the telephone. A minute later Bony was speaking to Pierce.

'About those footprints, Pierce. Did your tracker see them?'

'Yes. Why?'

'Did he make any comment?'

'No.'

'He accepted them as Yorky's, you think?'

'Must have done. He didn't say they were not Yorky's. Why?'

'Well, they aren't Yorky's. The abos here tell me they are not, and they should know.'

'But . . . I don't get it, Inspector.'

'I don't yet. The job was done well enough to deceive the men here, and yourself, but they didn't trick the abos. I understand that not one of the local abos saw those tracks at the time. Correct?'

'That's so. We put 'em all on the hunt as soon as possible.'

'All right, leave it for now. Another thing. If I don't contact you by six tonight, come out here. I've given myself a difficult assignment. There is a sugar sack deposited in Mr Wootton's safe which must be returned to the owner should anything happen to prevent me contacting you after six.'

'Sounds grim. Who's the owner?'

'The contents of the bag will tell you that. Be on hand, I'll ring again at six. I'm in the position of the man who, having tried to push the house down, has decided to blow it up.'

NINETEEN

EXTRACTING INFORMATION

CANUTE, KING of the remnants of a past civilization, had the game sewn up. Not for him a crown wobbling on an uneasy head. Not for him financial worries, domestic worries nor the problem of 'keeping up with the Joneses'. Like his ancestors, Canute knew all the secrets of living without heart disease or stomach ulcers.

This afternoon he reclined at ease on an old bag spread in the shade of a wattle, and chewed tobacco. A small boy was shooing away any stray ant, and the chief lubra was baking yabbies caked with mud and buried in hot ashes. It was a beautiful day, in dark shadow; a wonderful existence for a man. It would have remained perfect had not a remembered voice said:

'Take a little palaver with me, Canute.'

The King sat up, drew his feet under his thighs, grunted his displeasure. The little boy ran off to the lubras now standing amazed that the big-feller policeman had entered camp without their awareness of his approach.

'We have yabber-yabber, eh?' suggested Bony. 'You tell Murtee and that old fellow who is your eyes, and the other old men. Then we all yabber-yabber, eh?'

Canute shouted, and from various deep shadows men stretched and yawned, belched and muttered, momentarily froze on seeing the visitor squatting beside their Chief, and obeyed the order. The visitation was accepted as a tribal affair, and the King was led to his throne and his advisers grouped themselves about him.

The case brought by Bony the previous day was still there, and he seated himself and again, with slow deliberation, fashioned a cigarette, lit it, and stared at each man in turn. There was Canute, heavy from easy living, grey of hair and beard, still powerful, probably still under seventy. There was his eyes, a very old white-haired and white-bearded man named Beeloo, who was a human lath and crippled, but mentally on top. There was Murtee, the Medicine Man, about forty years old, savage of aspect, still savage in mind, his tongue pierced and his body carved with flints, as befitted the holder of such office. Finally, there were six other men, all older than sixty. Not one had attended a whitefeller school.

'You tellum those wild abos go back to camp?' Bony asked; and Canute nodded, on his face a sullen expression, ill-fitting his normal jovial nature.

'You smoke for them again, and you all be sorry,' threatened Bony. 'Which feller not go walkabout up to the Neales? Come on now, you tell pretty quick.'

'All blackfeller went walkabout that time,' declared Canute.

'You cunning feller, eh? Which blackfeller come back quick; come back look-see Mrs Bell lying dead outside kitchen door?'

'No blackfeller do that,' replied Murtee.

Bony expelled smoke, gazed at chattering finches in the tree above, deliberately inhaled and again blew smoke in a thin blue line. Ebony idols regarded him with shuttered eyes.

'I look-see find Yorky and Linda. You say big-feller policeman no find Yorky and Linda. I say you know all the time where Yorky and Linda are camped. You say: "Go to hell." Now I go crook. Whitefeller law is more strong than blackfeller law. What for you not tell the lubras and the young men where Yorky and Linda are camped? What for you all cunning fellers like this? Mrs Bell wasn't a lubra. Yorky isn't a blackfeller. Linda is a white child. Nothing to do with blackfeller law. You tell, eh?'

No movement. No speech. Graven images in human flesh. Bony persisted.

'One blackfeller stayed in camp that time you go walkabout, or he came back pretty quick. He went to homestead. He saw Mrs Bell dead on ground. He saw the blood mark on her back. It was like this.' With a stick Bony drew the mark of interrogation. 'He wait here till you all come back from the Neales.

He didn't send up smoke about Mrs Bell because he knew Mr Wootton and the men thought all blackfeller off on walkabout. Okee! All right!

'You all come back on trucks, perhaps. I don't know properly. But, when Canute and Murtee come back, that blackfeller who stayed in camp and saw Mrs Bell told about her, and showed Canute the mark on Mrs Bell's back. He held Canute's wrist like he's doing now, and made Canute see that mark. You, Beeloo, was blackfeller who saw Mrs Bell dead. Well, you now tell me about Mrs Bell all dead, eh?'

Not the flicker of an eyelid.

'Okee! All right, you-all! You know big old red-gum, your treasure house? I find magic churinga stones, and head bands, and magic Kurdaitcha shoes, and pointing bones. I find all them. What you-all say to that?'

That defrosted them. Murtee leaped to his feet, stumbled when Bony's automatic was directed to his paunch.

'Sit down, Murtee. You-all sit down. Feller that gets up till I say so is pretty quick dead. I am big-feller policeman. Whitefeller law. You try fight whitefeller law you get shot pretty damn quick. You listen.

'You Orrabunna fellers all finish. I took away the treasure, the pointing bones, everything. I lock' em up. Black-feller law no good any more.'

The loss of their tribe's treasure was devastating. Minus their magic stones, their precious heirlooms of human hair, their ancient dilly-bags, and the all-powerful-with-magic pointing bones, they were divested of family, of tribe, of origin, almost of being. As Bony had said, without command of their treasure they were as nothing. There sat the white-feller law. Death looked at each from that pistol, and now all protection from the white and the black laws was withdrawn from them. They were naked, defenceless against their enemies that had been kept at bay by generations of forebears with and by that hoarded treasure.

It was a body blow that Bony hated to deliver, and not for an instant would he have done so, had it not been for Linda Bell. Those shuttered eyes, the stubborn minds, were barriers not to be surmounted by bribes, threats, persuasion, argument, or even physical punishment.

'I have other pointing bones,' snarled Murtee. 'I kill you. Short time, long time, I kill you.'

Bony puffed cigarette smoke, lifted his upper lip in a magnificent sneer.

'Wind, Murtee. Strong-feller wind. Pointing bones I took, more powerful than your other pointing bones. I point the bones back at you. You die slow time, long time. Then you-all die.'

Livid fear mastered them, tautened every lip, tensed every muscle.

'We trade, eh?' said Bony softly.

Canute dashed drops of sweat from his forehead. Murtee seemed to shrink into himself. The ancient man shook, but his claw-like hand continued to grasp the Chief's wrist.

'What trade? You say,' pleaded Canute, and Murtee shouted. He attempted to stand, but his neighbour hauled him down. It seemed that Murtee's protest strengthened Canute, and the others nodded as though he could see their support.

'You tell about Yorky and Linda, I give back your magic treasure.'

'Okee, all right.'

'I give back your treasure and Murtee not point the bone at me, or any whitefeller.'

'Okee, all right,' agreed Canute; and the others, including Murtee, nodded agreement.

'You tell all about Yorky and Linda, and I get treasure from lock-up at homestead, pretty soon, quick, eh?'

'We seal it,' Canute said, and Bony drew on the ground between them two interlocking circles. The ceremony of the intermingling of blood followed, then Canute ordered the ancient who was his eyes to speak. His English was so light that a translation is given.

'I am a very old man, but still active about the camp. I could not go so far on walkabout as the Neales River. When the tribe went walkabout, I go bush. My heart is heavy. I am old and lonely. By and by I come back near homestead. I hear

133

Mr Wootton shoot crow, and I say this is strange, because this day Mr Wootton he go to Loaders Springs. I sit down long time. Then I get up and look-see out over lake, and I see Linda and Yorky out there on walkabout.

'I think Mr Wootton gone off to Loaders Springs, and I go on to homestead see if Mrs Bell give me tobacco. I tell her the tribe left me behind, and I am lonely and my heart is heavy.

'When I come to homestead, I don't see Mr Wootton. I don't see any feller. Plenty of crows, though. I go round back of men's quarters. No one there. All the men away. I see something on ground near kitchen door. By and by, I go over and see it is Mrs Bell. She's lying on her stomach. She is dead. I see the blood on her back. Then I run like hell, and all day and the next day I see the mark of blood on her back. Long time I think I go bush. Then I know the tribe is back in camp and I come back, too. I tell Canute about Mrs Bell. I tell about Linda.'

'Did you see Mr Wootton's car?'

'No.'

'Or the dust of his car on the way to town?'

'No.'

'You tell lies, eh? If Yorky and Linda walkabout on lake, whitefeller see their tracks,' taunted Bony.

'Yorky wear whitefeller Kurdaitcha shoes. Yorky follow dingo pad. Yorky not leave clear tracks. Whitefeller don't think to look for Kurdaitcha marks on dingo pad.'

'Good! You speak true. What Yorky do out on lake? He go right over other side?'

'Might be he camp along little-feller sand dune.'

No matter how he probed this last statement, Bony made no further progress relative to this point. The curtain had been lifted just a little to reveal the purpose of that discarded case board he had found outside Yorky's last camp. The whitefeller's Kurdaitcha shoes were certainly shoes for walking on mud. The 'little-feller' sand dune could be a tiny area of sandy-dry land in the sea of mud, the summit of a mountain in the mud sea, as the Pacific Islands are mountain tops rising above the ocean. The picture was clear enough, but the reality was to be questioned. Bony asked:

'Why didn't you tell all this to Constable Pierce?'

The answer was good and sufficient. Canute said:

'Ole Fren Yorky white-blackfeller.'

'Now you, Beeloo, you tellum truth. You say no one at homestead that time you find Mrs Bell dead. Who did you see near the homestead?'

'Yorky and Linda.'

'Who else?'

'Saw horseman way up on rise.'

'Pine tree rise?'

'Other side of homestead. Long way 'way. Going like hell.'

'Who was he?'

'Don't know. Long time. Long . . .'

'Could be a mile,' interposed Canute.

'What colour was the horse?'

'Not look. Much dust that day. Just horse and white-feller.'

'When you saw the horseman, where were Yorky and Linda?'

'Way out on the lake, like I told.'

They sat on the ground like so many squat idols on one side of two blurred circles, the circles representing the gulf between ancient and modern Man. There remained much to be explained. For instance, there was the crucial point of contact between Yorky and the aborigines during those periods when Yorky must have collected food.

Who met Yorky with the tucker? Had he to go to the camp for it? What had he told the aborigines of the motive behind the shooting of Mrs Bell? These questions yielded little save the impression that Yorky had given nothing away from which anyone, like Pierce or himself, might gain.

'Okee! All right! We finish trade, eh?'

Canute smiled with infinite relief.

'You come with me to homestead, Murtee. I give back your treasures.'

The two men walked the track to the homestead. Neither spoke a word. Bony's mind was occupied with the horseman riding from Mount Eden long after Wootton had left for

Loaders Springs. He wasn't Arnold Bray, who was driving a truck that day. He was Bill Harte, or Eric Maundy, or Harry Lawton. If not one of these men . . . It had to be one of them.

Wootton was waiting in the doorway of his office, watching the approach of Murtee and Inspector Bonaparte. He saw Bony nudge the aborigine, frowned with perplexity when they both turned and skirted the house and walked up the rise to the pine trees. They stood there for a few moments during which Murtee indicated with out-flung hand a point on the long rise on the opposite side of the homestead.

Arrived at the office, Bony asked for the sugar sack from the safe. Before parting with it, he stood calmly staring into the dark inscrutable eyes of the Medicine Man.

'You big Medicine Man,' he said, adding: 'I big-feller policeman. Perhaps you are not a cunning feller. Perhaps you just a bloody fool. I find out that Canute see blood mark on Mrs Bell's back. Canute tell me about that blood mark. He tell me with dijeridoo. Perhaps you all bloody fools. Perhaps Yorky didn't kill Mrs Bell.'

TWENTY

THE WAGES OF BLUFF

MURTEE STALKED away over the bare track towards the homestead gate and the camp. Bony called to Charlie, and when Charlie reached him, he loudly called for Sarah. The cook emerged and divided her attention between the departing Medicine Man and Bony, who said:

'Come with me.'

He took them up to the pine trees and told them to sit beside him. There was silence while he rolled the inevitable cigarette.

'Now will you tell me everything I want to know,' he said smoothly. 'There will be no more backing and filling. You don't understand, but no matter, that all you aborigines have been bricks in a wall I have battered down. Now I tell you something else.

'Remember those tracks I made at the veranda steps? Same tracks that were found behind the meat-house, and which every whitefeller said were Yorky's. Someone else made those tracks, to make believe Yorky made them. I find out that old Beeloo didn't go walkabout that time. He came to homestead thinking to get tobacco from Mrs Bell after Mr Wootton left for Loaders Springs. He saw Yorky and Linda walkabout on the lake, and he saw a horseman galloping up the rise back there. That horseman could have been the feller who made those crook tracks at the meat-house. He could have killed Mrs Bell.'

Sarah's eyes were now blazing black opals. Bony went on:

'That horseman was too far away for Beeloo to see who it was. If the feller on that horse killed Mrs Bell, then why did Yorky clear out with Linda? You tell me, eh?'

'One of them sums the Missioner asked us kids,' Charlie

grumbled. 'If it takes two minutes for a boomerang to go round in the circle in a north wind ... Something like that?'

'Yes, Charlie, something like that. Sarah, I'm telling you this because there's a good chance that Yorky didn't kill Mrs Bell. That's a good reason why we must catch up with Yorky. Supposing he didn't kill Mrs Bell. All right, then Yorky took Linda away, and if Linda died after he took her away, then Yorky is going to jail for a long time. That's why you must tell me all you can.

'Now Beeloo saw Yorky and Linda out on the lake, and he says that Yorky must have been wearing whitefeller's Kurdaitcha shoes. Remember, Charlie, I showed you a board out at Yorky's camp, and you wouldn't say what it was. I know now. It was a board for Yorky to walkabout on the mud.'

'That's true,' admitted Sarah. 'Yorky wore them boards when he had to work on the fence where it goes little way into the lake.'

'Then he could go out a long long way along a dingo pad wearing those board shoes, couldn't he?'

Sarah nodded, her eyes now like garnets. She shook her head when Bony asked if ever she had gone with Yorky far out. Sensing opposition building to meet further questioning, he asked:

'What's out there? Dry land?' They looked at each other, each waiting for the other to answer. 'I'll tell you. There is dry land out there.' Their eyes showed relief when Charlie said:

'Bad place out there, all right. Pretty near the middle. Nothing only sand and a bit of scrub. That's what Murtee says. He's been there, but no one else has, or won't tell.'

'Anything to eat?'

'Plenty of rabbits. Along one side, so Murtee says, there's a long waterhole with fish in it, and ducks nesting all about.'

'A good place for Yorky to hide up with Linda, eh?'

'You sure that Murtee not telling lies?' inserted Sarah. 'First time I hear of that ole place.'

'You're a lubra,' Charlie told her loftily.

'Yair. I'm a lubra. One time I'll choke that Murtee.'

138

'One time Murtee point the bones at you, and you fall down and grab your stomach and die. Murtee is plenty powerful.'

'That will do,' commanded Bony. 'Charlie, would you make me a pair of Kurdaitcha shoes to walkabout for Yorky?'

'Too right. When d'you want 'em?'

'By tonight.'

'Okee. Boss let me work in carpenter's shop?'

'He will. That sun's getting low, Sarah. What about dinner?'

They went down the slope to the homestead, where Sarah entered the house to fence with a wildly curious Meena.

Having showered and changed, Bony found Wootton in the living-room.

'That little scheme of mine paid dividends this afternoon,' he said, sitting with the cattleman. 'Will you be talking to your neighbours after dinner?'

'Probably. Why?'

'Could you arrange with them to listen in to a broadcast at five tomorrow morning?'

'Yes. What's it all about?'

'Who is your oldest neighbour; been living out here the longest?'

'People named Petrie down on the south of the lake, I think.'

'I'd like to talk with them tonight. Would you contact them?'

'Easily.'

Meena appeared, to set the table, and the cattleman knew something had happened from her excited eyes and energetic movements. He was frowning at the polished tips of his leather slippers when Bony asked if he would loan him a rifle.

'Of course,' he replied. 'I've a Winchester .44 and a Savage .25.'

'The Savage. It would be lighter. Who are your nearest neighbours to the south?'

'The same. The Petries. Their homestead is about a hundred miles from here. Well in financially. Two sons working there, and generally half a dozen white stockmen.'

139

'I don't remember the place,' admitted Bony. 'Must have passed by on my way up when I skirted the lake. Track, of course?'

'Yes. You go up the long rise to the old homestead where the Murphys once lived. You know, the people from whom I bought Mount Eden. On from there to the bore where young Lawton met you the other day.'

'That day Mrs Bell was shot, Arnold Bray was sent to the old homestead for iron?'

'Yes, that's so.'

'Does he do much riding?'

'Very little. You're damned mysterious this afternoon, Inspector.'

'I'll tell you something. You will recall that I said it was possible for one of you five men to have returned here that morning and murdered Mrs Bell. After you left in your car that day, a man was seen riding hard from the homestead up the rise and heading for the old homestead. I am rather curious to know who he was.'

'Is that so?' drawled Mr Wootton. 'Then one of three of us five could have ridden back and shot Mrs Bell?'

'Don't take me too literally. That rider could have come from the Petries' station. He could have had nothing to do with shooting Mrs Bell. He might have come on a legitimate visit, found Mrs Bell dead, and rushed away in a panic. I have made certain plans, and you will learn something of them this evening when we talk to the Petries and arrange tomorrow's broadcast. Dinner seems to be served.'

Wootton's excusable curiosity was unallayed by Bony during dinner and, immediately afterwards, Bony left the house and sought Charlie, who had returned to the carpenter's shop.

The aborigine had fashioned the mud shoes and fitted to them leather straps, and Bony now tried them on, finding them most awkward.

'Not that way,' Charlie told him. 'You slide 'em. Sarah show me; I show you.'

'Good! I'll have to get the knack. Remember that dog-pad

140

we saw half a mile from the pines? How many more pads like that nearby?'

'One more – at the hut on the boundary. Two more up by the Neales.'

Charlie agreed to keep watch on the pad near the homestead, as from after dark, to inform Bony if any blackfeller went out to warn Yorky. Later, for an hour, he talked with the surrounding neighbours over the transceiver, and, indirectly, gained much useful information about the country, and nothing whatever concerning the centre of Lake Eyre, save that it must be a bog even during the long period of drought. Still later, Wootton became interested in certain preparations. The Savage rifle was checked, ammunition poured into a small calico bag, dry biscuits and tinned meat brought from the store, and an old rucksack Wootton remembered having for several years.

Bony slipped away from the house and sought Charlie, who was faithfully on duty at the appointed dingo pad. The aborigine reported having seen no one on that part of the beach, and Bony sent him home to his bunk, and himself cat-napped the night away until just before dawn.

It was five o'clock when he and Wootton sat before the transceiver, and Bony began his broadcast. He said:

'It is now six weeks since Mrs Bell was shot here at Mount Eden, and her little daughter vanished. You all know of the extensive and the intensive search which followed. You know that it is strongly suspected that the man who killed Mrs Bell and abducted her daughter is a locally known identity named Yorky. From information received, and following the results of my own survey of the country, I have reason to believe that somewhere in the middle of Lake Eyre is an area of dry land forming an island in a sea of mud, and that the man Yorky escaped to that island, taking the child with him.

'Also from information I have gathered, I think it is feasible for a man to cross the mud to that island by following one of the dingo pads, when wearing mud shoes. By this means I intend to test what are as yet only theories. I intend to try to reach the island by one of the dog pads from near this homestead, starting within an hour.

'I have been informed by the aborigines that these dog pads are not numerous. They are certainly not easily discernible. Assuming that there is a dry area of land somewhere towards the centre of the lake, then we may accept as fact that the dingoes use the place to gain food or rear their pups. Picture that dry area of land as the hub of a wheel, and the dog pads as the spokes of the wheel.

'To reach the hub, I must follow one of the spokes, and, should Yorky observe me approaching, he might well leave for the shore by one of the other spokes. Therefore, you will appreciate my difficulty in apprehending him.

'I ask you to co-operate with me by arranging among yourselves to watch Lake Eyre. In view of the length of the shoreline, it will be difficult for the number of men available to watch all points, so we can only do our best. I do not anticipate contact with the wanted man until late today. I am sure you will realize how delicately this operation must be carried out. Our main objective must be the safe recovery of Linda Bell, if alive. I leave the risks to your imagination.

'Finally. There is to be no shooting unless a life is in grave danger. I want you to understand clearly that I am far from satisfied that the man Yorky actually did kill Mrs Bell. I feel that I can rely on your common sense, and know I may rely on your co-operation. Thank you.'

Bony faced about from the transceiver to regard calmly Wootton's outside staff, his inside staff, and the cattlemen, who turned about with him.

'I have something to say before I leave. You have just heard me broadcast that I am not satisfied Yorky killed Mrs Bell. That he and Linda Bell are somewhere out on the lake, I am hoping to prove within hours. Two matters cause me to doubt that Yorky is our man. One is that tracks found behind the meat-house and thought to have been made by Yorky are now proved to be forgeries. Thus they were made by someone wishing to incriminate Yorky. The other reason is that on the morning that Mrs Bell was killed, after you men had left on your duties for that day, after Mr Wootton left for town in his car, a horseman was seen riding away from this homestead.'

142

Sarah had provided early morning tea for the hands, and when all were in the kitchen, Bony telephoned Constable Pierce and spoke for five minutes. Ten minutes after that, he started out for Lake Eyre.

TWENTY-ONE

THE SINK OF AUSTRALIA

THE SUN rose above Lake Eyre, and it was like facing car lights ten yards distant. It was no hindrance to Bony, who had to concentrate his attention on the whitefeller Kurdaitcha shoes, fashioned so differently from the soft feathers worn by that fabulous creature. But the sun masked him completely from Wootton, who stood on the white beach, as well as from others standing high among the pines. He found that weight related to the area of the boards attached to his feet was not sufficient to clog the footwear if he proceeded by sliding one foot forward, then the other, and at the beginning of the journey the dingo pad was quite easy to see.

Progress, however, was slow. Muscles unaccustomed to particular stress began to tire, so that, on glancing back, he was dismayed on estimating that his voyage over The-Sea-That-Was was but a mile begun.

A hot wind was strengthening from the north, and it seemed to enshroud him in isolation completely foreign to that experienced on 'dry land'. One cannot be completely isolated when trees are neighbours, and sand dunes are dwellings, but here was nothing of the comfort of familiar things. Here was menace to spur imagination, to emphasize the hopelessness of help in distress; pictures of himself slowly engulfed by dark and evil mud, or trapped by monstrous things, flashed across his mind.

Grimly he went on when he longed to go back.

The dingo pad was seldom more than twelve inches wide, and often was reduced to four inches. At some places it was quite distinct; at others only a good tracker could follow it. When he was three miles from shore, the pad wound about a great deal, which aroused his interest, because, under normal

144

circumstances, a travelling dog proceeds straighter than does a man. Presently the pad became less twisted, and gave him his first surprise ... a narrow strip of hard sun-baked mud.

He was glad to remove the boards from his feet and pause for a smoke, and it was something of a shock to realize that his interest in these surroundings had subjugated the purpose of the journey. Where the pad met the dry patch, the dogs had scratched their paws clean of mud.

Having rested, he returned to the pad, noting once again that his board tracks were exceedingly light, and when examining the depressions with his fingertips, he learned that the resilience of the mud would within hours entirely obliterate them. That the pad itself remained clear was due to the number of dogs that had used it since water covered the mud so long ago.

This dry patch of only a few yards wide and a hundred in length was a resting place, as he himself was using it. The marks of claws on the hard surface proved that. It was perhaps four miles from the shore, now distorted by the mirage creating wide rivers in the declivities, and vast lakes between the slopes of gibber-covered uplands. Vast sheets of 'water' lay about, the mud surface visible only within a radius of half a mile.

Not only dogs, but crows had rested on this 'island' in the mirage. And not only crows had stayed a little while, gone on. Two spent matches told of human visitation. The matches told him nothing but that ... which was most satisfying.

To leave this patch of hard land was as easy as to arrive, there being only the one pad. Refreshed, Bony fastened the mud shoes and continued along this highway of the dingoes, the mirage receding before him, and ever flowing after him, the immediate surround always the same – flat, uniform of colouring, the top surface lifted to brittle pieces of crisp mud crust. A journey deadly monotonous, were it not for the little mysteries.

Why did the pad turn sharply to the right, continue in that direction for a quarter mile, again turn left, to continue the overall course to the east? Why did it proceed for three miles more straight than a man-made path, and then zigzag over a full mile? There was nothing which could be seen to account for this.

The day wore on, and he was beginning to wonder what kind of night he would spend if he had to camp on this narrow dog pad, when again the pad angled sharply. It had reached the border of a large area pitted by open holes the size of a florin. The dogs had not crossed it, had skirted it, and he saw why when a green finger emerged from one of the holes, beckoned to him, sank again into the mud. Then while he watched, other green fingers appeared, beckoned, and disappeared.

Curiosity was suddenly submerged by desire to get away from this place of the unknown; the beckoning fingers became the miasma of a nightmare, and the board shoes the leaden feet of it.

An hour later he was thankful to reach another patch of bone-dry mud, to rest and take stock of his progress. The sun said four o'clock. There was no landmark, and how far out in the lake he had come it was not possible to assess.

This hard patch was about an acre in extent, and having rested his aching muscles, he strolled over it and found evidence of a dingo rest, and again the spent matches. Of human tracks there were none, the ground being too hard to register any.

He decided to spend the night here, although he could not dismiss from his mind those sinister green fingers. He was less concerned by his food supply than by the three pints of water he now carried in the canvas bag.

Since daybreak he had consumed one pint, and, despite the aid of the pebble he had sucked all day, he felt this was the minimum for existence. The aborigines could live for a week and more on half a gallon of water, but not D. I. Bonaparte with his preference for countless cups of tea.

Until the sun went down, it was not possible to see land, and Bony occupied time by testing for water under the mud. He had found a short swathe of tree debris, among which was a

146

four-foot stick, and although he didn't find water even by seepage, he did uncover the mystery of the erratic course of the dingo pad. The true bottom of Lake Eyre was not flat, as the surface of the mud overlay indicated, but rather was similar to the sea bottom, with its valleys and hills and mountains. The dogs followed the summit of ridges, and the two areas of hardened mud merely covered the tops of subterranean hillocks; and that area of mud from which upthrust those extraordinary green fingers must mark a valley or chasm.

The mirage ebbed, to form long silver strips, and these shallows disappeared slowly, to vanish entirely when the huge red fireball tipped the distant uplands. There was the land ten miles away, and there was an object three miles away which certainly was a moving human being.

Seated on the hard mud, his arms clasping his knees, Bony watched and waited for the being to identify himself. Slowly colour faded from the sky, and the lake revealed all its true starkly drab and loathsome self, from which the sky blenched. As the minutes passed, the figure on the mud appeared to be no nearer, and yet was following the pad by which he had travelled. The dusk deepened, and there was no skyline, no background to gain a silhouette and so learn whether the person was white or black.

When half a mile from Bony, when he could dimly follow movement, the figure stopped, stood for a few seconds, finally sank to the pad. It was obvious that the man did not know of this second resting place, and had decided to park himself before darkness blinded him to the depths of mud either side of him.

For a space, Bony lay on his back looking at the unwinking stars, only those of the first dimension able to penetrate the high level haze. Restless, he sat again, smoked cigarette after cigarette, being careful to shield the flame of matches, and knowing it wasn't his match flares that had determined the follower to walk that pad in the dark.

He heard the impact of mud with shoe one minute before the figure emerged from the darkness to reach the island in the mud and give vent to a sigh of satisfaction. The figure

stooped to unstrap the boards, and then its identity was re
vealed.

Bony chuckled.

'Welcome, wife!' he called. 'Welcome!'

He advanced, struck a match, saw the dark eyes meeting hi
own above the tiny flame. She stood silent, waiting for repri
mand, making no movement when he slipped behind her and
eased from her back the rope slings holding the laden suga
sack.

'Your eyes are better than mine, Meena, but I am sure you
legs ache more than mine do.'

'I thought you would be angry,' she said, and obeyed when
he suggested she sit with him. 'Are you?'

'Not at the moment. Why did you come?'

'Yorky has a rifle.'

'I have, too.'

'Yorky is a dead shot, Inspector.'

'You may call me Bony. I am a dead shot, too.'

'Yorky might kill Linda. I came to stop him.'

'Well, leave it. When did you eat last?'

'Before I left Mount Eden.'

'Then you must eat before you explain, and before I becom
angry, if I do. And, somehow, Meena, I cannot believe I shal
ever be angry with you.'

The starlight emphasized the vastness of this place in which
was no security against natural forces, no protection from un
known powers. The wind came softly, in fitful little gusts
bringing scents unknown to them, and strangely repellent
Presently, Meena said:

'What were those green things coming up out of the
mud?'

'Whatever they were, I feared them,' admitted Bony.

'Could be Carlinka,' the girl said, and when Bony pressed
for information, she went on: 'Story told by Canute. In the
Alchuringa Days three blackfellers out hunting met a gian
centipede. The centipede said: "Don't kill me. I'm Carlinka."
So they didn't kill him. They turned him over on his back and
scooped sand over him. They found they couldn't cover him

148

properly because his legs waved about so much, and then a dingo came along and said he'd help, and he did by scratching up the sand till all they could see of Carlinka was the tips of his feet wiggling about.'

The reddish light gleamed on her shoulders and naked breasts, her slim arms, and was reflected by her eyes. He knew himself to be old only in pride bidding him to remember not what he was, but who he was. When he spoke his voice was unnecessarily harsh.

'Now tell me why you came.'

'It's like I told you, true. Yorky has a rifle. So have you. You're a policeman, like Constable Pierce. You go after Yorky. When Yorky sees you and fires, telling you to go away, you won't because you're a policeman. You will fire back if Yorky doesn't give up. And he won't. And there's Linda. Sarah kidded Canute to tell about Yorky and Linda camped in the middle of the lake, and Canute told Sarah Yorky could stop all the policemen in the world from getting him. So I came to talk to Yorky. Better to talk than shoot.'

'Much better, Meena,' agreed Bony. 'Who made your Kurdaitcha shoes?'

'That Charlie.' Meena looked down and smiled. 'Me and Sarah told him. He wouldn't at first, but we made him. Sarah was in a tantrum. We found Charlie hiding in the motor shed, and after a little time he made the mud shoes for me, all right.'

'The men, what were they doing when you left?'

'They were all gone. Constable Pierce came and went away with Mr Wootton. Like you said on the radio, they went to catch Yorky coming off the lake. The men rode away before Mr Wootton. The men took their guns, too. I heard Harry tell the others to shoot Yorky on sight.'

The quivering voice was an entity fleeing away into the silence, and presently it came again.

'You don't know Yorky, Ins. . . . Bony. Yorky wasn't cruel to anyone. He never treated us aborigines like dirt. He was kind to everyone. He's the kindest whitefeller who ever was, not a dingo to be hunted and shot.'

'Are you sure it was Harry Lawton who urged the others to shoot him on sight?' pressed Bony. And when she answered affirmatively, he said: 'Take it easy. We have to be on the dog pad at first sight of dawn.'

TWENTY-TWO

THE CORPSE OF THE PAST

THEY WERE four miles on to the east when the sun blotted from that quarter the endless rusty mud and began hastily to lay the mirage over the putrescence of its own creation. It had been comparatively straight going, proving the dogs followed submerged ridges, when sharply the pad turned left towards the north and away from the glaring sun. Minutes later they saw movement at about half a mile, and stopped.

'What is it?' cried Meena, who was close behind Bony. 'I don't like it.'

A something rose and subsided erratically, never in the same place, and, without replying, Bony proceeded with his rifle more easily accessible to hand. They could see the lake floor was moving, and ultimately the pad skirted this area of disturbance. Great mud blisters rose and sank without bursting, the light glinting on them as though the skin was stretched taut with pus. There was no evidence indicative of thermal forces agitating this area of several square miles of turbulence.

'Go on, Bony. Don't wait here. I don't like this place,' Meena urged.

Far away something rose above the general level which was no blister. It was like a wave running end-forward, then abruptly it turned towards them and drew close in zigzag fashion. It suggested the movement of a great reptile swiftly passing under the mud which rose to curve away from its back. There was certainly no solidity anywhere except that under their feet. The wave thing skirted their end of the area and slowly sank among the recurring blisters.

'What's doing it, Bony?' Meena whispered, but Bony merely shrugged and pressed on. What could he, the big-feller policeman, say in answer to so simple a question? How to explain something apparently behaving in opposition to natural laws? How to explain those green fingers? Or to bring logic to bear on the rotting corpse of This-Sea-That-Was?

The pad skirted the area for more than a mile, and twice the whale-like bank of mud rose and moved with astonishing speed as though the mass were a living thing. Merely a quarter mile from them, a hill of mud rose many feet, to disintegrate as though from internal combustion.

The sky was white, the sun itself tawny, and the wind came to hurry them onward to safety from this blistered menace. A possible explanation, in Bony's opinion, was that this area of deep mud was agitated by water pouring into the northeast section of the lake, thus creating pressure and stress, and were this so, then danger to themselves was to be reckoned with.

He gained another opinion later when skirting a small area of liquid mud bearing distinct traces of oil. The wind then was so strong that the surface was ridged with sluggish ripples.

When the sun was searingly hot on their backs, they came to the next dingo rest. Both were physically exhausted and disturbed by the implications of the mud's behaviour, for should the water rise to cover the surface, the dog pad would disappear, and they would be engulfed.

'Two hours ago I urged you to go back. I do so now,' Bony said, and all the reaction he produced in the girl was a slow smile and a negative shake of the head.

'Yorky and Linda are somewhere out here,' she reminded him. 'And I wouldn't go back past those things for anything. You don't seem to mind, though.'

'I mind all right, Meena. I'm not liking this at all.'

'I know. If there was a wall of fire half a mile on, you'd go straight through it instead of going back. The Missioner told us that pride goeth before a fall. I hope you don't fall.'

'We haven't that kind of pride, you no more than I. You and I are merely animated shells crammed with fears and inhibitions, humility and pride. What white people might name courage is in us instinctive revolt against the abyss for ever opening at our feet. We must not fail. We dare not think of failure. So we must go on, even if we have to travel right across this abominable lake.'

152

They ate slowly. Sips of water immediately issued from them in the form of perspiration, the natural bodily function having ceased since leaving Mount Eden. For a little while they lay with their faces pressed into folded arms to give relief from the glare to eyes sore and heavy.

'You don't really think Yorky shot Mrs Bell?' Meena asked without raising her head.

'No. But don't ask me why he bolted with Linda. I couldn't answer that.'

'D'you know who did shoot her?'

'One of two men, possibly. It could be one of five men, but I think it's one of two.'

'Which two, Bony?'

'It is now three hours to sundown, Siren. We should press on and hope to reach another dog rest before darkness stops us.'

'All set. I'm ready.'

She was lacing her mud shoes when he raised himself and blinked against the fierce light. He offered to carry her store of food, but she refused. She stood straight and strong, and the beauty of her body defeated the grime and dust and mud flakes adhering to it. Over her deep-gold face was the smile again, a smile of daring, with a dash of inscrutable woman.

Now and then she watched him pushing on ahead, seemingly making light of the gear he carried and finding no difficulty with the boards, and, as with their maternal forebears, both possessed that rare ability of closing their minds to physical discomfort and concentrating only on the important matter of arriving.

They came to a break in the pad of several yards, and after tentatively testing the surface, managed to cross by hurrying. Another area was pocked by mounds two feet high, and from the mounds came sucking and gurgling sounds. Bony, having heard and seen the giant earthworms of Gippsland, wondered how enormous must these worms be, if worms did produce the sounds and the surface casts.

Often he expected the water to flow around them, and as often was fooled by the mirage, so complete was this trickery played by Lake Eyre. Four crows came from the east, mocking them as they passed. That morning he had noticed three flying to the east, and as he laboured onward, he speculated about the additional bird.

When the sun went down, the wind was furnace-hot, the sky a flaming fire, and the surface of the lake was a red-gold sea. Far ahead tall masts towered to the sky, and from tip to tip of these masts sped something resembling nothing. Abruptly there appeared an object looking like a crab walking on the edge of its shell.

'That's them,' shouted Meena, and Bony turned to say:

'Could be. But how far away?'

The question baffled her. The shadows of the voyagers magically lengthened and were barely the width of a hair. The flame of the sky darkened to crimson, and the mirage turned to green and swiftly from green to steel. Overhead the crimson pall quivered, became ribs of blood veined by black valleys and moving ever to the east before the wind; the mirrored surface of real water to the north enflamed by the setting sun.

They could see the gradual darkening as the sun passed over the rim, and swiftly all the colours under the sky faded into drab brown oblivion. Quite suddenly they saw, barely two hundred yards distant, a low wall of reddish sand, topped with tussock grass. And a man and a child!

'Down,' shouted Bony, as he sprawled forward on his chest, wriggled slightly to pull the rifle off his back and bring it to the ready.

Facing the glare of the western sky, the man and child sighted the voyagers moments after they themselves were seen. Yorky, for it must be he, flung himself down behind the robust tussock grass, but the child continued to stand on a miniature hummock of sand.

The moments were those between the magic hours of day and the shrouding hours of night, when this country is revealed in true perspective, and this evening, stereoscopic clarity. Over the barrel of his rifle, Bony watched the movements behind the grass, and actually witnessed the muzzle of Yorky's Winchester being pushed through the fringe.

A swift glance backward showed him Meena still standing, and he called to her to go down. She shook her head and shrilly shouted to Linda:

'It's me! Meena! Tell Yorky, Linda. Tell Yorky!'

Meena provided a perfect target. Bony, who was better than average, could see the tip of Yorky's rifle and knew precisely where the man's head was in relation to it. The range was only about two hundred yards. The light held. Perspiration ran like rain down his face to wet the stock of his rifle against which his cheek was pressed. If Yorky fired first, Meena or himself would die. If he fired first, curtains for Yorky. Instinct drove him to pull the trigger; training commanded him to wait.

TWENTY-THREE

A MIXED RECEPTION

BONY WAITED.

A lesser man might not have hesitated before speeding a bullet into Yorky's brain. He would act on the impulse of survival of the swiftest, and subsequently would be commended for preventing the possible murder of the woman so rashly exposing herself to danger.

Great men are natural gamblers. Bony gambled that Yorky wouldn't shoot his own daughter; and that Yorky wouldn't shoot him, not yet. He believed that Yorky thought himself behind full cover, and therefore safe from destruction and in command of the situation. And, like all great gamblers, Bony won. Linda shouted:

'Come on, Meena. Tell that man to stay there.'

Above his sigh of relief, he heard Meena sliding along the pad, and when the sound stopped and he heard her panting, he said:

'You will have to step over on me. Do it quickly.'

'That Yorky!' she exclaimed, almost crying. 'That ole fool of a Yorky! I thought you'd shoot first. Why didn't you? Why? He could have killed you easy. I'll fix him.'

He felt the board press lightly on the small of his back, its toe-tip dig into his neck as she stepped over, regained her poise and stayed to look back at him.

'I'm all right, Meena,' he told her. 'Go on and pacify Yorky. Get his rifle if you can, but don't try fighting for it.'

Obediently, she went on along the pad, and Bony continued to hold his rifle sights at a point one inch above Yorky's rifle muzzle. That muzzle wavered not at all, informing Bony that it was aimed at him, and not the girl.

Even though concentrating on Yorky, Bony could see Linda dancing in her excitement as Meena slowly neared the sandbank. He heard the child's cries of joy, and the girl's rapid questions and command to Yorky to point the rifle elsewhere. Then she was on the narrow hard crust dividing sandbank from mud, and the child was in her arms. After a few moments, the child was running to Yorky, and Meena was removing her mud shoes. Obviously, Yorky issued an order, for Linda screamed:

'You man over there! You come here. Yorky won't shoot.'

Bony walked to the solid land with taut expectancy. On sliding to land he had an impression of fluffed water beyond the dune, and mud extending into blue-tinged darkness. Meena and the child came close to him, and nearby a man chuckled mirthlessly, and said:

'Linda! Take the rifle from that feller.'

The little girl's brown eyes stared up at Bony as she held out her hands, and Bony smiled.

'Thank you, Linda. I want to take off these silly boards. My word, I shall be glad to be rid of them.'

'Bring the rifle to me, Linda,' commanded the hidden Yorky, and Meena said sharply:

'Cut it out, Yorky. You're not on the films.'

'I'm a desperate man,' snarled Yorky, and Meena retorted:

'You will be if I get at you. Point that gun some other place. We haven't come to shoot you. You are all right, Linda darling? That Yorky! Wait till Sarah gets at him.'

Yorky stood at the edge of the sandbank, a small, wizened, sun-blackened man in working trousers and shirt so repeatedly washed as to be negative. His greying hair was over-long, and the grey moustache suspended long tails to the tip of his pointed chin. His eyes were light blue, small, and red-rimmed. The Winchester still pointed at Bony.

The culminating surprise of this day was the contrast between the hunted and the hunters. Both Yorky and the little girl were clean and tidy. Yorky had certainly shaved that morning. Bony could not forbear gazing from them to Meena and himself, then back to Linda, and laughing.

'Linda, who looks the dirtiest? Meena or me?'

'You do, lying out there in the mud like that,' replied Linda severely. 'But we have a private lake, you know. We can have a bath whenever we like, can't we, Yorky?'

'Yes, I suppose so,' agreed Yorky, and a further surprise was the faint whine in his voice. 'Comin' barging in like this. How'm I to know you didn't come to get me? Anyhow, who are you? Ruddy stranger to me.'

'I am a person of little importance,' countered Bony. 'Linda mentioned a lake, and that indicates water. We have been severely rationed. Where is this lake?'

'Over there,' shrilled Linda. 'I'll show you. Come on.'

Following her pointing finger, they saw the steely sheen of water seemingly close enough to step into, and Bony, with Meena, who was being dragged along by the eager Linda, heard Yorky say:

'Now look-see, Linda. You've been in there all of two hours already. Don't you be going in again, or you'll be getting a cold or something.'

There was the water, inviting, alluring, limitless now in the deep dusk. Linda shouted. Meena shouted. Bony shouted. Meena stepped down from the sandbank to the bordering hard ground, stepped into the water and, finding the bottom hard, went farther in, splashing as the water rose to her waist. Bony followed her. Behind them the little girl and the man were silhouetted against the pink sunset sky.

Water in the middle of Lake Eyre! Water in the centre of a near desert at the end of a rainless summer. Clear water, and fresh, and seemingly miles of it lying cool and sweet under the serene stars and the flaming meteors.

When emerging to be met by the impatient Linda, Meena was even more beautiful, but Bony, still wearing shirt and trousers, looked like a near-drowned cat. Pulling off the shirt he wrung it out, thankful that it was cleaned of mud, and after all the surprises of this day came another when Yorky said:

'Better come on up and have a drink 'er tea.'

The invitation belied Yorky's hostile attitude. Stepping back, he motioned them up on to the sand-bar, Linda leading the way to a shallow dell where a small fire burned before the dark opening of a grass humpy. Beside the glowing embers stood a billycan, and close by were fruit tins for cups and one filled with sugar.

Linda ran into the grass shelter and came forth with a towel, which she presented to Meena, who quickly dried herself and passed the towel to Bony. Shorts and trousers began to steam in the fire heat, and Linda expertly poured tea into two tins, and went again to the humpy, this time returning with a dainty cup and saucer.

Juggling the hot tin in his hands, Bony turned his back to the fire to face Yorky, who was sitting on the ground several yards away, and stubborn yet with the Winchester ready for action.

'You answer questions?' demanded Yorky, the whine still in his voice. 'You march into my camp without any by-your-leave. You don't say who you are. Why?'

'Sorry,' Bony said. 'I've become so accustomed to asking questions that I find it tedious to answer them. Now listen to me.' Authority had crept into the cold accentless voice. 'I am Detective Inspector Napoleon Bonaparte, of Queensland, assigned to locate the whereabouts of Linda Bell, and apprehend a man concerned with a crime of violence. Having found Linda Bell, I have yet to apprehend the slayer of you know who. Now, suppose you answer a question? You tell me why you cleared out from Mount Eden and brought Linda with you.'

Yorky advanced until he was within a yard of Bony, the rifle aimed at Bony's chest. The firelight gleamed in his eyes made small by suspicion.

'Suppose you tell me what you're driving at?'

'I'll answer that one, Yorky, by suggesting that talking of serious things be deferred until Sleepy Head has retired for the night.'

'That don't satisfy me,' snarled Yorky, and Meena cut in shrilly:

'No, it wouldn't, Yorky. You told Linda all that happened?'

'No, I haven't yet.'

'Then shut up and put the rifle down. We're famished.

Where's our packs, Linda? There's tinned stuff in one of them for sure.'

They disappeared in the direction of the 'beach', and Bony said, proceeding to push fire sticks together:

'I don't believe that you shot Mrs Bell.'

'But everyone else must,' replied Yorky.

'I don't.'

'You don't! D'you know who did?'

'My guess is good. Had you shot her I'd have had the cuffs on you before now. Easy man easy! They are coming back. We'll talk of other matters. Do you know that the floods are pouring into Lake Eyre?'

'They are? Bad?'

Yorky sat in the circle of firelight, placing the rifle at his side. He was still suspicious, and almost furtively began to chip flakes from a plug of tobacco.

'Down the Coopers and the northern rivers.'

'You see water on your way?'

'No. But there was the mirage of water in the sky. You must have seen that.'

'Didn't think.' Yorky fell to watching Meena opening tins. Linda appeared, this time carrying two large dolls, one the image of Ole Fren Yorky, the other that of Meena. She began to croon to them.

'We saw strange things,' Bony went on. 'That great slough of soft mud is being agitated. Could be caused by water pressure building up underneath it. Did you see it?'

'Didn't travel that way since we come out here first. The mud was quiet enough then. Must be the flood,' agreed Yorky. 'Have to shift camp first thing after daybreak.'

'Where to, Yorky?'

'Where to! Don't know, exceptin' back to the shore.' In the ensuing silence the only background sound was Linda's crooning voice.

'There is another way to the shore?' asked Bony.

'Yes, the pad I take to the old hut at the south end of Mount Eden boundary fence. Much shorter. I've been back there twice for tucker.'

'You must have been to the homestead at least once, for the dolls?' pressed Bony.

'No. Friend of mine brought 'em from the homestead.'

'Friend of yours!' echoed Meena. 'What friend?'

'You stop askin' questions,' whined Yorky. 'Just a friend, that's all.'

'Did you meet this friend, or did he leave the dolls in the hut?' pressed Bony.

'Left 'em in the hut.'

'And this friend didn't leave word that the water was pouring into Lake Eyre?'

'No. Musta forgot.'

'Must have forgotten! He would know that the water would cut you off, that you'd starve to death, or drown trying to reach shore, wouldn't he?'

'Yair, I suppose he would,' admitted Yorky. 'But . . .'

'And he forgot to leave word. Nice friend, Yorky.'

'Damn nice friend,' jibed Meena, and Linda said sharply: 'It's rude to swear, Meena.'

'Must of forgot,' obstinately averred Yorky. 'Anyhow, we'll have to move in the morning. Linda, you be off to bed. We got a long way to go tomorrer.'

'But you haven't told my nightie story yet,' protested Linda. 'You always do, Yorky.'

'I know, but not tonight. I'm too sleepy tired.'

'I'll tell the story,' volunteered Meena. 'Now you show me the inside of your little house. Come on!'

Linda gathered her dolls under one arm, and picked up the cup and saucer. Politely, she wished goodnight to Bony, threw her arms round Yorky, and said he must go to bed, too. With additional interest Bony studied the nondescript little man who had abducted a child and cared for her exceedingly well under hazardous conditions. The humpy constructed with tussock grass thatched to a frame of driftwood accepted the little girl and Meena, and after a short silence Yorky said:

'That right you reckon I didn't shoot Mrs Bell?'

'Did you?' countered Bony, and Yorky sighed like a man long and sorely perplexed.

161

'I was sozzled and all on the boss's whisky. I don't rightly remember, but I must have. Things happened sort of out of order. You said you got a different idea. What do you think?'

'While not quite certain,' Bony tersely replied, 'I think your friend did.'

TWENTY-FOUR

THE QUAIL SHOOTERS

WITH DWELLERS in the Outback, it is often the rule to wake by habit when the first sign of coming day appears in the sky. Such a bushman was Yorky, who stirred from his bed of sand and added wood to the still red embers of the camp fire. The resultant flame enabled him to see the empty billycan, and he departed for water. On his return he found Bony cleaning the Savage rifle, and while waiting for the water to boil he watched Bony at work on the high-velocity weapon; and neither spoke nor made a move to halt the progress.

Having tossed a handful of tea into the boiling water, Yorky lifted the billycan with a stick, and cut chips from his plug while waiting for the leaves to settle. Thus the day began completely normal.

Having cleaned his rifle, Bony set it carefully against his pack, and nonchalantly strolled away to wash at Linda's own lake. Meena and the child joined him there, and all returned together. The Savage still reclined against the pack. Yorky hadn't touched it. Smoking his first pipe of the day, Yorky ambled over to the water, and Bony finished dressing, simply by donning an old coat over the now dry shirt.

They were ready to move before sun-up, by which time Bony had surveyed their immediate surroundings and learned that the tussock-covered sand was barely a hundred yards wide, and in varying width extending as far as he could see to the north and south. The 'private lake', enclosed by sand, was about an acre in area, and must be maintained by springs.

They left the soft sand for the narrow beach, where Yorky led the party to the south. An hour later, when he halted for a rest, they were still walking the beach, and still the sand-bar was on their one side and the mud on the other. Now well beyond the place of recent occupation the rabbits were fairly numerous, and already two dingoes had been seen.

'How much farther have we of this easy going?' Bony asked.

'About another seven miles,' replied Yorky. 'Nearly all them seven miles towards the shore, for this sand takes a turn like the elbow of a boomerang. That leaves only about eleven miles of mud. There's water at the end of the sand, but not like Linda's lake. After that no water till we get to the hut. How you going, Linda?'

'All right, Yorky,' replied the child, a trifle doubtfully.

'Expect I'll have to carry you a ways. Easier on this hard beach than later on over the mud. Mind you, Linda, sweetheart, you're doing good, but them legs of yours are too short and them Kurdaitcha shoes aren't much good for the job.'

The shoes Charlie had made were slung about the child's neck by the leather thongs. They had been fashioned with the bark of a tree to the shape of a boat, or like an Eastern slipper, having a curved toe-cap. They were too long for Linda unless she was also wearing her normal shoes, and, in fact, were not meant to be worn save in play. The yellow comb of a white cockatoo adorned each shoe immediately behind the raised prow. Along the sides of each shoe Charlie had scored aboriginal pictures, and glued to the raised edges were the herring-bone feathers of emus. Toy shoes made for a little girl.

'I shall be glad to be on the mud,' observed Bony. 'That friend of yours could have decided to meet us, and could be waiting comfortably behind a clump of tussock grass.'

'Who's your friend, Yorky?' demanded Meena. 'I'm tired of you not tellin.' Looking back at Bony, and noting the slight frown of anxiety, she went on: 'You wait. Sarah'll get it out of you. You say you didn't do it. Bony says you didn't do it. Bony says your friend did it. Wait till we get back to Sarah, Yorky. She'll make you talk fast enough.'

'That feller didn't do it, I keep tellin' you,' exploded Yorky. 'He's been pretty decent all through. Only one I could trust, anyhow. And I'm not talking until we're all facing him. Then we'll see. I'm not a one to talk behind a friend's back.'

'All right!' exclaimed Bony impatiently, for he had spent an hour the previous night arguing this point. 'But we're not

164

taking unnecessary risks. I shall walk well ahead, and if he is waiting for us, I'll try to flush him from cover. You are being extremely foolish, although it isn't vitally essential that I know the name of your friend at this moment. Nor do I need your co-operation.

'Before leaving the homestead, Yorky, I broadcast my intention of hunting you here, and by now the lake is being patrolled by men waiting for us to make shore. I made no secret of our ability to walk the mud by following the dingo pads. And I let it be known that I do not believe you are guilty of murder.

'Broadly, that was the situation when I left the homestead. The guilty person anticipated that you would be cut off by the flood water, then he would always be safe. Now that he knows he isn't safe from the consequences of his crime, it is most likely that he'll attempt to stop us returning. Where better to do that than somewhere along this sandbar? He could drop one of us, and take his chances in a duel with the other man. Better than inevitable arrest. This pal of yours, does he know of this shorter route to the shore?'

Yorky had been staring at his boots, and now he gazed steadily at Bony.

'You done it purposely, drawing the killer out here?'

'I did,' replied Bony. 'This rifle is able to out-range any Winchester. I gave him the chance to come here and fight it out because of that, and because I thought I'd have you to back me up. Now that you won't, then I'll go ahead and take the risk of being dropped before I can locate him.'

'You said you guessed who done the killing,' argued Yorky, eyes small and hard. 'Why didn't you arrest him before you started?'

'It's a long road between knowing and proving.'

Again Yorky stared at his boots, and Meena watched, silently, Linda cuddled against her, tired and fearful from this, to her, inexplicable conversation. Abruptly, Yorky stood and, without looking at them, said:

'You got it all over me, but I'm stickin' to me guns. I could be ratting on a mate. You and me'll go on ahead of Meena and

Linda. We'll take equal chances. You're the Law. But law or no law, anyone starts after Meena and the lass, I shoot and keep on shootin'. We got to get off this flamin' lake, and quick. She's startin' to heave already. I can see it.'

Looking over the mud, at first they saw nothing unusual.

'You're referring to that moving ribbon of reflection, are you?' asked Bony

'Yair, that's it. I've never seen it before, but the abos got a name for it. It's a low sort of swell, and the sun's glinting on it along one slope, like a water wave. Old Canute told me about it. The water keeps on pushing into the mud, and instead of running over the top of the mud, it comes up from under.'

Yorky turned to the girls.

'Drop all your traps. Me and the Inspector'll carry 'em. You take the shoes, Inspector. I'll carry the water-bags. Dump the rest. Meena, you tarry awhile. Give us half a mile lead, then come on.'

'Okee. Don't worry about us.'

'My dolls!' cried Linda. 'I won't leave my Meena and Ole Fren Yorky.'

'We'll carry them, Linda,' soothed Meena.

'Keep to the beach,' instructed Bony. 'Any firing, crouch down against the sandbank.'

The two men spaced themselves and advanced along the bar, their weapons ready for instant action. They could see for several miles above the grass and the wind-fashioned hummocks of sand, and less than fifty yards ahead into the grass or over a sand hump. It wasn't dissimilar from stalking quail, but anticipation of action was certainly based on far different conditions.

The good general projects himself into the mind of his opposite number, and Bony tried doing just this. It would be unlikely that the killer of Mrs Bell would delay his first shot one moment after the distance between him and them fell below two hundred yards. The odds were grossly in favour of the ambusher dropping one or other of his adversaries, who were under the compelling urge to get clear of the lake. Just too bad if he manoeuvred himself so that they both passed him before he fired.

Fortunately it was a calm morning, and the stiff tussock grass was still. They held a slight advantage given by the eagles and the rabbits, and by four crows which had followed them from the camp. The crows often flew on ahead, but certainly would behave erratically did they see a man prone on the ground beneath. It was easier to watch them than the eagles, two of which were flying high.

An hour passed. Yorky constantly glanced across at Bony, keeping abreast. The sun was rising to the zenith and the heat was powerful. Bony thought of Linda, argued whether to make a halt or not. On looking back, he could see the upper portion of Meena, and the head of the little girl above the edge of the bank. They were keeping distance very well. He called to Yorky:

'Leave one of the water-bags on the beach for the girls.'

Yorky nodded and the march proceeded, each man zig-zagging in short legs, each tensed to dive for cover at any instant, Yorky also watching the birds and working widely with Bony when the sandbar widened.

An hour before noon, Bony fancied he could see the extremity of the sand, and he was laying odds in favour of the ambusher waiting there, when just ahead of Yorky a pure golden dingo appeared on the top of a sand hump, saw the men, and loped away, followed by four well-grown pups. Bony sighed his relief.

Having decided that Meena and Linda hadn't halted at the water-bag to eat and leave scraps the crows came on after the men, passing them, and flying on over the dogs. The end of the bar, now clearly seen, was perhaps half a mile distant, when the four crows arrived there, and swept skyward as though from a ground explosion, and at height swirled like black snowdrops. Their cawing came to the men, and the tale was told.

'That's him sure enough,' shouted Yorky, and converged to Bony. 'We gonna move on like we done in the blasted war?'

'Yes,' agreed Bony. 'We can each keep to a beach to gain

partial cover. Now for the drill. Although I don't look it, I'm a law officer. Although you don't look it, you're an Australian citizen. Our job is to get that fellow alive, and he isn't going to be much use to you dead. So, unless you are pushed badly, don't shoot to kill.'

'Suits me.'

'Back to the beaches,' cried Bony almost gaily.

There they gained two feet of sandbank cover, and yet were able to mark each other's progress. The crows were circling over the end of the sandbar, their suspicion prolonged by an object lying prone, and their behaviour brought low the two eagles, soaring in gigantic circles, with seldom a wing flap.

It was then that the enemy knew he was sunk, and his nerve, what there was of it, failed. Two men stalking him when they should have been walking blithely into his gunsights. He could both see and hear the damned crows betraying him to the men, one of whom was reputed to be the finest rifle shot in the back country.

Hastily strapping on his boards, he slithered over the dog pad, watched by the fearful dingo bitch and her curious pups. On Bony and Yorky reaching the end of the sandbar, which was fashioned like a crab's claw about a small sheet of gleaming water, the mirage had given him stilts.

The disappointed eagles rose to cooler altitudes. The crows were decidedly annoyed. Bony sat down and produced tobacco and papers.

'That your friend?' he asked.

'How do I know?' replied Yorky. 'With your rifle I could drop him. Got better range than mine. That particular bastard means nothing to me.'

'To the contrary, he means very much to you,' insisted Bony mildly.

'That bloke's still in range. He'd have got one of us, and then if he'd got the other he'd have killed the lass and Meena. Gimme that Savage.'

The Winchester was aimed at Bony's chest, and casually Bony set down the Savage on his far side.

'Meena and Linda would see you shoot me,' Bony explained.

'That wouldn't do, Yorky. Load your pipe instead. I know how you feel on being betrayed by one you trusted. Who is he?'

Yorky shook his head, and the stubborn perversity of his class came out when he said:

'You're a policeman. I can't inform to a cop.'

TWENTY-FIVE

PINNED LIKE A SPECIMEN

HAVING RESTED for almost an hour, chiefly on account of Linda, Bony led the party on to the mud, the pad clearly marked by the impressions of the boards worn by the retreating ambusher. It was then one o'clock, and Bony pointed out the advisability of reaching land before five, after which hour the westering sun would blind them, but not the man who might decide to stage a battle from the cover of a sand dune.

The child was subdued, but walked a full two miles before complaining. Then Yorky demonstrated that little men are often physically stronger than larger men. He passed his rifle to Meena, took Linda astride his shoulders and carried her as though her weight was identical with that of the weapon. The afternoon was exceedingly hot, completely still, and the surrounding mirage dazzled the eyes and limited shooting visibility to eighty yards.

Having insisted on a lead of two hundred yards from Yorky and the girls, Bony constantly peered ahead, worried by the fact that, as time passed, the sun would place him at increasing disadvantage. The crows had refused to follow the party, preferring no doubt to take shade among the foot-high grass, and now to look to the sky for the eagles was torture to sweat-rimmed eyes. Above and about there was nothing but colourless light.

On reaching an area of hard ground, he waited for Yorky and Meena, and eventually they appeared, first as tufted masts, and then walking on stilts, and became normal only when within yards. Yorky was still carrying Linda, and on setting her to ground, he stumbled to his knees and sprawled forward, wiping his sweat-drenched face on a bare forearm.

Meena poured water over the back of his head, and he told her to stop it, as they had yet five or six miles to reach land.

Thereafter they all drank sparingly, and the men smoked little, the terrific heat pressing in from all sides equally with the direct rays of the cosmic sun. Yorky did spare water to saturate the towel which Linda wore for head covering.

'That'll be better, sweetheart,' he told her gently. 'It isn't far to go now, and when we get to the hut we'll pour buckets-full of water over each other.' To Bony he said: 'On a bit there's another dog-rest. It's small and only a couple of miles from the shore. It'll be there that bloke will be waiting again. After that there's the shore dunes for him and open spaces for us. Then the fun'll start. It'll be all his way with the sun behind him.'

'Maybe not,' Bony said. 'I'll get along. Give me time. I'll wait on that dog-rest if he isn't there.'

Yorky brought his wandering eyes to focus on Bony. They were inflamed, and like agates set in beef.

'You forget you're a copper. Just remember you got a Savage what'll out-range a Winchester, and remember that we got to get off this stinkin' mud before it bogs us. This ain't no time for the ruddy Law and gentlemen policemen.'

'Correct, Yorky.' Bony smiled grimly. 'The water under the mud is the boss from here. I'll be waiting at the next rest.'

The man and the woman and the small child watched the mirage shape grotesquely the departing Bonaparte, and Meena said angrily:

'You shouldn't of said that. You got us all in this mess, and he knows what he's doing without you telling him.'

'Had to chiack him,' retorted Yorky, glaring at his daughter. 'Me, I can look after meself. But we got our little Linda sweetheart. Well, up we come and off we go.'

*   *   *

The heat was relentless and Bony was dismayed by experiencing a slight attack of giddiness. He thought perhaps he had been moving too fast, and slackened his pace a little to recover. He did, until minutes later, when he had another attack that almost sent him down.

It was then he saw it, the slow passing of a mud wave. It

caught stronger light along its forward face than along its summit and rear, bringing foreboding of disaster. Half an hour later another mud wave tended to upset equilibrium, and then soon after that a wasp buzzed, and he heard the report which sent him chest-down into the mud, and his eye peering across the sights of his rifle.

'You've said it, Yorky. This is no time to be a gentleman,' he remarked. 'Let me see this murderous swine that I may prove it.'

The frustrating light was much worse at mud level. He could not determine where the mud horizon met the scintillating atmosphere. Again the wasp fled by, and again came the report loud and sharp. He aimed at the point of the sound and fired, and the report of his rifle seemed to be blanketed about his own ears. It was worse than being blinded by fog. Irritation gave place to dull anger, and anger banished all veneers, leaving a man no longer a gentlemanly copper.

There arose, in this man of two races, emotion he rarely permitted to surface. It was like a heatless fire deep behind his eyes, and he swore at the blinding sun and the frustrating mirage. Pinned like a moth to a specimen board, he and those behind him were being vitally delayed for the mud to engulf them.

Ah! There was movement of a sort, a shape impossible to identify. Swiftly it grew to monstrous size, swiftly to diminish to vanishing point. The sniper was retreating.

Bony made to leap to his feet, and was brought to reality by the mud shoes. He wanted to run, but again the boards restrained him. In a semi-crouching attitude, Bony hurried after him, with the nightmare sensation of leaden feet.

He came to the dingo-rest where the sniper had staged his last hold-up, and instead of waiting for the others he pressed on, determined to nail the enemy before he could gain cover behind the shore dunes. Now how far to the blessed land, the clean, the beautiful land? How much farther over this filthy mud? What had Yorky said? Ah, yes, two miles. A long way, and yet not so long when clean red sand and a hut near water waited.

172

An hour later he saw the red sand, sand rising in billows as of red spray suddenly suspended, great red cliffs of it, gouged and gullied by the shadow drifts of graphite powder. And he saw, without distortion, a man run from the mud and race up the beach. Without expending time sprawling, Bony halted, sighted and fired. He heard himself shout when the running figure staggered. He heard himself curse when the running figure recovered, to run on between two cliffs of red spray.

He was down on the mud yet again, fighting for control of breathing and nerves. He struggled to sink yet lower into the mud, knowing that his adversary was calmly selecting his cover from behind which he could pin down a regiment. How far was he from the beach? It was impossible to assess distances in this shimmering colourless radiance.

His rifle was ranged to fire point-blank up to 350 yards. He could do nothing now but wait, hoping to see the spurt of flame before hearing that wasp, thus learning the position of the adversary. Vain hope, indeed, when the sun is directly before one, and a bare five hands' width above the summits of low dunes.

He was thinking how to place himself beyond range of the Winchester and still keep the dunes within range of his own rifle, when a sound like a cork being withdrawn came from his left, followed about two seconds later by the report. To turn about and retreat in a manner dictated by mud and hampered feet was to ask for a bullet in the back from a man able to see clearly with the sun behind him.

The next bullet hit the mud several yards immediately in front of Bony. He saw the tiny spurt of mud so disturbed, and found consolation in the obvious fact that the marksman could not see where his bullets hit, and so correct his errors, for the impact raised no dust. The following bullet informed him that the marksman was immediately to his front, and probably behind a low declivity between two humps.

To his complete bewilderment, therefore, he witnessed the appearance of a dark figure at a point at least two hundred feet to the right of this place; and the figure was a man who was waving something white. Then in the shimmering light haze he saw that the man was moving in a crouching manner along the foot of the dunes, and towards the place where the rifleman should be. Bony aimed at this position and fired, and was rewarded by the miniature avalanche of sand marring the face of the dune.

Now there was distinct movement on the top of the ridge between the dunes, and two things happened. A bullet plopped into the mud on Bony's left, and the man at the foot of the dunes began to run, still crouching, towards where the marksman must be. He was stalking the rifleman, and had taken advantage to cover ground when knowing that the marksman was concentrating on his shooting.

Good man! Bony proceeded to assist him further by now and then claiming the rifleman's full attention. The stalker entered a shadow, disappeared. A bullet plopped into the mud eighteen inches in front of Bony's rifle muzzle, and he realized that, fortunately, bullets did not ricochet off mud. Then he saw the white fabric being waved atop a sand ridge much nearer the marksman, and Bony tried to dig a furrow across the ridge.

Minutes passed. The sun sank lower still, even more effectively blinding Bony, who could now see only by shading his eyes. Shortly afterwards even that was useless. Lying there utterly helpless while the sun sank behind the sand ridge were moments suspended for ever. Now the distant land was sharply silhouetted against the light; for the first time the odds were in Bony's favour. The shadows were gone, the light shimmer was banished. He could see clearly the scar of the avalanche made by his bullet on the virgin face of the dune behind which lurked his adversary.

Then he saw a movement directly over his sights, and settled to make this a victory shot, stilling his nerves, freezing his arms and neck muscles while beginning the slow pressure on the trigger. This was it. He could actually see the top of the fellow's head over the smaller blob of rifle muzzle resting on the sharply etched red sand line against the saffron sky. He knew now that the range was well under two hundred yards, and in his hands was a superb weapon. Conditions were ideal.

Now to dispatch a high-velocity bullet into the brain of the killer!

One fraction of increased pressure on the trigger and the bullet would have been sped, one fraction of a second more would have achieved finality. But the second passed and the pressure was stopped, for just beyond the marksman rose that waving white object. It rose above the ridge, revealing the head and body of the man waving as he mounted the opposite slope. The man lifted his arm, and his hand held a rifle or a waddy. Whichever it was, it was brought downward with severe force.

Then on the summit was an aborigine waving vigorously for Bony to come on.

Reaction almost caused Bony to sob from sheer frustration. He wanted to shout oaths and curses. Having waited all that time, having exposed himself to bullets all about him, having come to the moment of equalization, to be frustrated by a damned abo!

Standing, he sloughed the mud from his clothes, and congratulated himself that there wasn't a smear on the rifle. Turning about he saw Yorky and Meena still far out, the man continuing to carry the child, and when the storm of unreasoning anger subsided, he placed the rifle on the mud without a qualm and went back to meet them.

'He pinned me to the mud,' Bony said. 'Just when I was able to let him have it, that blasted aborigine clouted him.'

Yorky, standing like Atlas, screwed his face into a peculiar expression, part admiration, part incredulity.

'You pinned him behind that sandhill, too, for a full hour. I'd sooner be talking to Linda than lyin' where you was. Better get going, Inspector. This mud'll turn to soup any minute.'

'Let me carry Linda. Edge round me and go first. That aborigine . . . I must admit . . . is our friend for life.'

'It's Charlie,' Meena said, quietly, and with infinite pride. 'He's still waving.'

Yorky headed the short procession, swaying drunkenly with fatigue, and followed by Bony with Linda astride his shoulders. The mirage vanished into the miasma of nightmare, and the land of salmon-pink urged them off the rusty-iron Lake Eyre.

'I don't want to see that ole lake again.'

'Neither do I, Linda. I like lakes with cool water, like your private lake out there. And when I reach a shower I'll stay under it all night.'

'You can't. Mr Wootton wouldn't like you wasting all that water.'

'Wouldn't he?'

'No. Mr Wootton is a careful man, my mother says.'

He set her down on the hard beach, and thankfully removed his mud shoes. Yorky and Meena were looking up at the laughing Charlie standing on the sand ridge, a white handkerchief about his neck.

Behind the ridge a white man sat with his knees hunched and his face resting on his arms. There was blood on the crown of his head. His rifle lay a dozen feet away, a Winchester.

'Is this the friend you were telling us about, Yorky?' asked Bony, and the little man looked vaguely about before nodding.

TWENTY-SIX

BREACHING A WALL

BEFORE THE dominant sun rose again, Bony was writing his report on the veranda at Mount Eden. He was wearing steel-blue silk pyjamas under a sky-blue dressing-gown, and although he had spent a full hour under the shower late the previous night, he had this morning showered again, and carefully tended his straight black hair.

At six a.m. through the french windows came Meena with tea and biscuits, and Bony found it difficult to reorientate this young woman wearing a white apron over a bright green dress, and red shoes clip-clopping on the veranda floor, with that girl in the once-white shorts who had accompanied him across miles of scabrous mud.

'Good morning, Meena! You're looking delightfully fresh this morning. And how is Linda?'

'Like a crane with its head under a wing.' Meena smiled her own indescribable smile, which would live for ever in Bony's memory. 'Looks like she'll sleep all day, too. What will happen to her?'

'Well, from what Mr Wootton said last night, I believe he intends to adopt Linda.'

'Make her his own little daughter! Oh, that'll be beaut. Then she'll be staying here for always?'

'Excepting when she will be away at school in Adelaide, and that will be some time ahead. Is Sarah happy to have Yorky back?'

This time the smile ended in gurgling laughter, and Meena managed to say:

'That Yorky! He was sitting in the kitchen after supper, and Sarah was all talk, talking at him. Suddenly he was fast asleep, and d'you know what? She picked him up like he was

Linda and carried him to her room and put him to bed. And crying all the time, after all she said she'd do to him.'

'And did I see you and Charlie holding hands on the truck last night coming back from that hut?'

'I had to let him for a little while. Then old Murtee told him to stop. He said didn't Charlie know I was your woman, that you bought by blackfeller trade with Canute. Went crook, ole Murtee did.' The smile began and quickly vanished. 'That Murtee's a bigger wowser than the missioner.'

'Now we are gossiping, Meena. Take away this tray and leave me to my writing. And don't forget that you are my woman, not Charlie's.'

Gazing into his stern face, so unbalanced by the twinkle in the blue eyes, she said with siren softness:

'I'm not arguing about that, Bony.'

Bony lit another cigarette, and discovered that concentration on the report demanded effort. He was busy, however, when Sarah tapped her iron triangle, and a few minutes later the cattleman called him to breakfast.

'Feeling better for a good sleep?' Wootton asked and, on being assured, added: 'What's the drill today?'

'After breakfast, I'd like to talk to everyone,' replied Bony. 'Might we have them all on the side veranda? Then we all go to Loaders Springs for statements to Constable Pierce. I told Pierce we'd be there at eleven.'

'We shall have to leave at nine.' Mr Wootton looked at Bony appealingly. 'About Linda. Think you could help by supporting my application to adopt her? We spoke of it last night, remember, and Pierce was keen when he went off with his prisoner.'

'As far as I know there are no near relatives entitled to claim her. However, the authorities would have to be sure that she would be cared for properly. I have no doubt you could give that guarantee, and later today I'll offer a few suggestions which should support you. Thank you, Meena, I'll have bacon and soft fried eggs. Never again tinned meat. And, Meena, close the door.'

Linda had fallen asleep too confused and weary to probe Meena's story of her mother having been bitten by a snake. She woke to find Bony sitting on the edge of the bed and nursing the replica of her mother.

'You are having breakfast in bed, Linda,' he said. 'Meena is bringing it. Afterwards, we are all going to town to buy a present for Meena. But that's a secret.'

'And see my mummy at the doctor's? Is she better?'

'I'm afraid not. It was bad. It was too late and everyone was away at the time.'

Bony offered the doll, but what Linda saw in his eyes and face caused her to twist aside the bedclothes and seek warmer comfort in his arms. When Meena came with the breakfast tray the shock had been cushioned, and he left the child being coaxed to eat her breakfast.

Passing to the side veranda, he found Mr Wootton waiting with all his staff bar one, who was within Constable Pierce's lock-up, and, having lit a cigarette, he said:

'It is not customary for an investigating officer to address all his original suspects at a gathering like this, but I decided to do so, chiefly because I've had to contend with grave obstruction built by loyalties.

'Loyalty, as you must know, is often in error, and is certainly not a virtue limited to one nation, one race or colour. About this you will agree as I proceed.

'On the morning that Mrs Bell was murdered, three men rode off to work on horses, one drove a truck for roofing-iron, and Mr Wootton left by car for town. When the men returned they found Mrs Bell shot dead, and Linda missing. It was a wild windy day, but they found tracks which they were sure were left by Yorky, and remember, before Mr Wootton returned and told them he had that morning found Yorky at the deserted aborigines' camp.

'Then it was automatically accepted that Yorky was the murderer. Efforts were made to track him, but not until late next day could aborigines be brought back from Neales River, and sent to track Yorky early the following morning. There was only one man in everybody's mind. Yorky. No other person was suspect, and so no other man's tracks would have been of interest.

'On my arrival, I found universal anger that the crime had been committed, but an almost unanimous good opinion of the man who was thought to have committed it. Everyone told me that Yorky was a nice fellow, and that his last bender must have sent him crackers. Opportunity for murder was present, the means were proved, but the motive was hidden.

'What gave me furiously to think was the behaviour of the aborigines. They lost interest in tracking Yorky, gave up before it could be expected of them, in view of the fact that Yorky is a white man and that he had taken away a white child. Yorky was said to be very close to them by long association, and, were this so, then it could be assumed that they knew where he was hiding. Effort to prove this assumption gradually achieved results. I was confronted by two tasks: to find the murderer of Mrs Bell, and to locate Linda Bell.

'I don't claim to be an anthropologist, but I do know that the aborigines in the central districts of Australia have been very much less influenced by the outside world than have the aborigines in the far north by the Melanesians and the Polynesians. These central Australian aborigines are being erroneously referred to as Stone Age men, when in fact they were thinkers and dreamers long before the Stone Age. The anthropological furrow ploughed across the Lake Eyre Basin by Spencer and Gillen at the end of the last century hasn't since been deepened by a fraction of an inch in furthering our knowledge of this, the most ancient race. At risk of being reviled by the alleged experts in this field, I admit that I gained my first lead in my investigation from Chief Canute and his dijeridoo.

'All the aborigines, so I was assured, were away on walkabout at the time Mrs Bell was murdered, and yet blind Canute knew the shape of the bloodstain on the dead woman's back. That the shape had been described to him by Yorky, or by any other white man, could not be seriously considered, because to a white man the shape would be relatively unimportant. Therefore, one aborigine did not go with the tribe on walkabout; one aborigine actually saw the body and the shape of the bloodstain, which he conveyed to Canute.

'I was compelled to employ unorthodox means of finding that particular aborigine. He is called Beeloo, a very old man for whom the walkabout was too much for his strength. Beeloo stayed behind and went a little walkabout alone. Coming to the day Mrs Bell was killed, he knew it was a Thursday, and that every Thursday Mr Wootton went to Loaders Springs. He knew that, save for Linda, Mrs Bell would be alone at the homestead, and he decided to ask her for a plug of tobacco.

'On reaching the homestead by his own devious way, he saw Yorky and Linda out on the lake, and he saw, too, a man riding away on the track taken by Arnold in his truck earlier that day. Unfortunately, distance, plus dust, plus mirage distortion, prevented him from identifying the rider or even the colour of the horse. He looked upon Mrs Bell's body, and then believed that Yorky was involved in the murder, and, finally, he knew where Yorky was heading to gain sanctuary.

'This adventure of Beeloo's was ultimately reported fully to Canute, and still I haven't yet answered the question of why Canute pulled his young men off hunting for Yorky. Yorky isn't a blackfeller, but Yorky was sealed into Canute's tribe and was married to Sarah by aboriginal rites. So Yorky, despite his colour, is one of themselves, and consequently entitled to their loyalty. That loyalty would remain even if Yorky had killed Mrs Bell.

'I was like a man bushed until I tested the prints said to have been left by Yorky and proved them to be forgeries. By whom? Not by Yorky, but by another who had planned to inculpate Yorky. That man must be he who was seen riding away. He was one of the three stockmen who had ridden from the homestead before Mr Wootton left, or someone from the station to the south of Mount Eden.

'At the time Yorky came back from town, I reasoned that he might know of the northern rivers in flood and yet be unaware of the seriousness of the flooding. I reasoned that the horseman seen by Beeloo would know where Yorky was going, would know about the flood-water sweeping into Lake Eyre, and be well aware of the probability of Yorky and the child being isolated on a sandbank in the centre, and therefore doomed. Lastly, I gambled that if he knew that I was to bring Yorky and Linda back from the lake, he himself would be endangered, and would make a move to stop us, and to disclose himself.

'I made that early broadcast so that that man would know my intention to seek out Yorky. The murderer had built an edifice to safeguard himself, and he knew it would crash to dust once I contacted Yorky.

'What he didn't know is that, had he remained inactive, he might have got away with murder for lack of sufficient evidence to put him into the dock.'

TWENTY-SEVEN

A PRESENT FOR CHARLIE

'WOULD YOU care to tell your story, Yorky, or shall I?' Bony asked.

The little man was sitting on the floor, with his back against the house wall, and beside him sat the enormous Sarah. Finding himself the object of general attention, Yorky swiftly looked down at his legs and was shaking his head when Sarah replied for him.

'You been tellin' stories goodo, Inspector Bonaparte. You tell em' better'n my ole fren Yorky.'

'Very well, Sarah. Yorky says that when Mr Wootton left him that morning at the camp, he started off for the homestead, but that shot of whisky given by the boss made him a little sleepy. So, before reaching the homestead gate, he slept for a period he cannot estimate, in the shade of a tree.

'Still jittery, he staggered on to the homestead, where he remembers seeing a saddled horse tethered to the yard gate, took little notice of it, and proceeded direct to the open door of the kitchen.

'There he heard voices within, voices raised in angry argument. A man was accusing Mrs Bell of encouraging him, and Mrs Bell was loudly denying anything of the kind. Not wishing to intrude or be discovered listening, Yorky dropped his heavy swag and leaned his Winchester rifle against it, intending to find Linda and talk with her for a little while. He says that when passing the office on the way to the playhouse, he noticed the key in the closed door, and remembered that Mr Wootton sometimes kept a bottle in the office. To use his own words, he was feeling "bloody terrible."

'I think that in Yorky's condition I might have succumbed to the same temptation. Anyway, Yorky entered the office and he found a bottle, a full bottle of whisky. He intended to take just one hearty nip and replace the bottle exactly where it was, but the nip was so hearty that the tide ebbed by one-third before he realized that a tiddler's mouthful was actually a whale's.

'He was sitting in the boss's chair, and talking to an imaginary companion, when he heard the shot. At first he thought it was the boss shooting crows. Then he remembered that Mr Wootton had gone to town. He decided he had better leave the office, and found difficulty in recalling exactly where the bottle had stood before the tide went out.

'Eventually he left the office and carefully closed the door, and I believe him when he says he was partially blinded by the sunlight, and that he didn't see Mrs Bell lying on the ground until about to trip over her body. He heard sounds inside the house, which, I've no doubt, was the transceiver being smashed. Befuddled with whisky, still a little blinded by the sunlight, he says he picked up his rifle and swag, and was intending to clear out, when Harry Lawton appeared and said: "By crikey, Yorky, what the hell did you shoot her for? You must be crackers."

'Such was Yorky's mental state that he gazed with terror at the weapon in his hands, then at the body. From the confusion of mind emerged one idea. His rifle was his dearest possession; he had cleaned it the morning before Mr Wootton had stopped at the camp, and now, sniffing at the muzzle, he could register the smell of the expended cartridge.

'He said, dully: "Yair, I must be."

'Lawton said: 'You killed her all right. I saw you fire. I rode over from the yard to see Mrs Bell about me lunch I'd forgotten to take out, and I saw you. I don't want to be mixed up with it, Yorky. You better clear out and keep going."

'Yorky panicked. He filled his gunny-bag with rations and cooked foods, and said he'd cross the lake to an island he knew of in the middle. Lawton asked how he was going to stay there without food and water, and Yorky told him there were rabbits, and that he could find water.

'It would appear that Lawton was greatly concerned about Yorky, and Yorky told him there were rations in the hut on the south end of the boundary fence. Lawton assured Yorky that he would replenish the food at the hut, that Yorky wasn't to worry. Just stay out on his island. And he had better take the kid with him.

'Yorky says that he argued against taking Linda, and that he was overruled into doing so. He was tormented still by the effects of a long carousal, partly revived by a small dose of whisky, and more than revived by too much in too short a time. We can imagine his state if we cannot wholly sympathize with him. Always a quick thinker, Lawton found it easy to think for Yorky, telling him that mates have to stick together, that he would do all he could to put off the trackers and the dirty coppers, and so on. "Yorky's good friend!"

'Lawton knew what Yorky in his condition did not know, that the floods were about to enter the lake. He foresaw that Yorky on his island would wake one morning to find it surrounded by water, and would be marooned there. And, finally, Linda opened two doors for him.

'Having shot Mrs Bell, he knew he would have to destroy Linda, for although the child had not appeared, he could not risk her seeing him cross to his horse and ride away. The shooting of Mrs Bell had been done in mad lustful anger. It was with cold deliberate purpose that Lawton determined that Yorky take Linda with him, for then she would drown with him.

'All this came out in his confession last night to Constable Pierce. He was a young man who ought never to live in conditions of such isolation – not without a woman. When he was stopped from interfering with the lubras, he stood on the brink of an abyss, when he turned his mind to the only woman at Mount Eden. I have no doubt his claim that she encouraged his advances was due to imagination. All the men absent, he returned to conquer by compulsion, and when Mrs Bell ran from him he thought she was running to Linda. About to rush after her, he found the swag with the rifle leaning against it, snatched up the rifle, pumped a cartridge into the breach and fired. Recognizing Yorky's swag, he wiped off his own fingerprints, and put the weapon back where it had been, and before finding Yorky, re-entered the house to smash radio and telephone.

'Now to tidy up the plan which almost evolved itself. Yorky said he would have to get his mud shoes. Lawton urged him to collar Linda from the playhouse while he went to Yorky's room for the boards. There was more quick thinking now when confronted by the desperate urge to get Yorky away with Linda. Obtaining the mud shoes, he met Yorky coming from the playhouse, carrying the child, and he hurried them round the back of the office to avoid the body. And, lastly, now knowing that the boss had seen Yorky, and in order to make sure it would be known Yorky was at the homestead, he obtained a pair of Yorky's old boots and made the prints for Bill Harte and others to see.

'Although Yorky could not remember shooting Mrs Bell, he was bullied into thinking he must have done. Lawton knew that his "frame" would collapse once I found Linda and Yorky. When he knew I was about to do that, he determined to prevent the four of us ever getting off the mud, and on learning from Yorky that the shortest track from his island came in at the boundary hut, he anticipated we would return that way. He had taken rations and the dolls to that hut for Yorky to collect.

'Now, Charlie, you tell.'

Charlie's round face rippled into a wide smile.

'Well, Inspector, you told me to fox Harry Lawton and do nothing only if he started shooting somebody. After you went out on the mud I was watching Harry, when Meena jawed me about making her some mud shoes for her to go after you. That Meena! Time I done them shoes for her, Harry and the rest have cleared out, and I asked the boss where Harry went. The boss said to Yorky's old fence hut down south.

'All the spare horses are gone, too, so I had to walkabout down there, and it's sundown when I came to the camp, and Harry's cookin' a feed for himself. Doin' what you said, just fox him, I has to do a perish that night, and next day late, when Harry mooches over to the lake sand dunes, I gets me chance at tucker in the hut.

186

'In the afternoon I seen Harry mucking about with case-boards, and I knows what he's up to. But he don't do nothing that night, and the next morning he's gone. I track him to the lake and see where he's taken to the dingo pad, but I can't see him 'cos the sun's in me eyes.'

Charlie burst into prolonged chuckling.

'There's me sitting like a crow on a windmill, and there's Harry out there with a rifle what I haven't got. I can't fox him on the mud, so I goes to the hut to get a feed and a drink. After that, I lie on the dunes waiting for Harry to come back, but he don't, and next day I decides I'd better get back to the homestead and tell the boss all about it, even if I been told not to tell anyone anything about Harry.

'I'm on me way along the beach when I hears shooting out on the lake. So I rushed back. Then I sees Harry well out. The sun's my way, and I can see he's coming to the shore, and fast. He's still got his rifle, so I burrows up and watches him. Then I see the Inspector comin' after him, a long way back. Harry gets to land, whips off his shoes and runs for the sand-hills. There's a shot and Harry gets it in his leg. He gets to cover and starts shooting, so I has to creep up behind him, and at the same time tell the Inspector it's me what's doin' the stalkin'.'

Once again Charlie broke into chuckling laughter.

'I got him okee all right. Right on the bonk.'

*   *   *

When the Mount Eden party left town for the Mission, Constable Pierce went with them. The Mission wore its Sunday atmosphere, for it was after four o'clock, and none of the children were in evidence. The doors of the little church were wide, and at the main entrance waited the Missioner to greet the visitors.

Between him and Bony with Wootton and Pierce was a short conference, then the Missioner entered the church, and Arnold said to Charlie:

'Come on, you. You're for it.'

Charlie, who was wearing a white cotton shirt and flannel

trousers, might have been going to the guillotine, and after he left there appeared the Missioner's wife, who brought a colourful garland of flowers which she placed around Meena's neck. Wearing a white silk dress, patterned with red roses, nylon stockings and white shoes, all of which Mr Wootton had that day bought for her, Meena recoiled with startled eyes on receiving this token of distinction.

'What's it all mean?' she asked Bony, who had slipped her arm through his own. 'You're married already. You told me.'

'By right, Meena, Yorky should be doing this,' he said, and Constable Pierce laughed and nudged Yorky. 'But as you are my woman, I have the honour of giving you away at your wedding. Everything has been arranged. Mr Wootton is going to build you a cottage at Mount Eden, so that you may keep an eye on him and Linda.'

Linda, wearing her favourite pink dress, smiled shyly at her pretty Meena.

The church was filled by the Mission children. Charlie and his best man were waiting, and the Missioner's wife was playing the organ. With Meena on his right arm, and Linda's hand on his left, Bony walked the one and only aisle.

Charlie was stunned; Bony presented him with the golden ring, which he was still admiring when Linda reminded him to put it on Meena's finger.

In the vestry Charlie and his bride signed the register, then Meena turned about to the smiling Bony, her eyes twin black opals, and flung her arms about his neck, kissed him hard and more than once. The astonishment of the onlookers turned to merriment when Charlie laughed so heartily that he had to regain control to shout:

'That Meena.'

If you have enjoyed this Pan book,
you may like to choose your next book from
the titles listed on the following pages

The Dain Curse 45p
Dashiell Hammett

'The talk is tough and to the point, the action is hard and fast, and the telling is swift and sure'

Oxford Times

One by one, those closest to Gabrielle meet violent, hideous deaths . . .

Through a mind clouded by drugs, she knows she is cursed.

As the slaughter assumes strange, cult-ridden shapes, one of Dashiell Hammett's toughest investigators comes to grips with a case that is either murderous conspiracy or modern witchcraft at its most evil . . .

'Nobody else ever did it quite like this, and no one has done it since'

Times Literary Supplement

If You Can't Be Good 45p
Ross Thomas

'Go-go thriller with absolutely smash finale'
Guardian

'There were days when I went for an hour or more without even thinking about sex . . .'

Decatur Lucas had uncovered some nasty scandals working for the government. Now he was hired to dig the dirt on ex-Senator Ames.

It looked like easy money until the senator's daughter crumpled to the sidewalk in a big charred knot . . . until Homicide moved in . . . until he met Connie Mizelle . . .

'Along the line enters one of the bitchiest young women in contemporary mystery fiction . . . Thomas does not spare the punches . . . fast-paced, brightly observant'
New York Times

'Hyper-compulsive'
Observer

Jaws 60p
Peter Benchley

'Pick up *Jaws* before midnight, read the first five pages, and I guarantee you'll be putting it down, breathless and stunned – the final climax is even better than the beginning – as dawn is breaking the next day'

Peter Grosvenor, Daily Express

The acclaimed new bestseller – soon to be a major film – of one man against a giant killer shark and a small holiday resort on Long Island that won't face the truth. Private feuds, lusts and jealousies take second place to a relentless duel almost unbearable in its suspense and danger . . .

'As engrossing a tale as you're likely to encounter until Hailey's comet comes round again'

Chicago Sun-Times